HEART STRINGS

BLACK MAGIC OUTLAW
BOOK THREE

Domino Finn

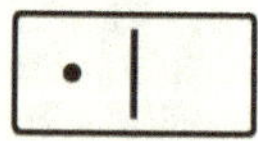

Copyright © 2016 by Domino Finn. All rights reserved.

Published by Blood & Treasure, Los Angeles
First Edition

This is a work of fiction. Any resemblance to reality is coincidental. This book represents the hard work of the author; please reproduce responsibly.

Cover by James T. Egan of Bookfly Design LLC.

Print ISBN: 978-1-946-00803-9

DominoFinn.com

Magic is Real

Not only that, it's all around you. Energies, events, encounters. Dark places filled with mythic creatures every bit as dangerous as their legends.

Opening your eyes to this reality isn't easy. Silvans are tricky. Vampires operate in the shadows. Even wizards greedily hoard their secrets.

What you need is an outlaw. Someone with nothing left to lose. A tour guide to the supernatural underground who packs enough grit and spellcraft to handle anything in your way.

What you need is Cisco Suarez, a hard-talking, hard-fighting, hard-luck hero.

Welcome to the exciting world of Black Magic Outlaw. It isn't always easy, but it's always a blast.

Previously in Black Magic Outlaw

The name's Cisco Suarez, and I'm a necromancer. It's all fun and games till you wake up dead in a dumpster.

Turns out, I'd been out of commission for ten years, if you can believe that. Not exactly dead, as the mysterious Covey put me under a vampire compulsion and a healthy dose of voodoo to make me their personal hit man. At least until my curse was broken.

Taking back my life means getting answers. Not simple, exactly, but straightforward - at least until I discovered my ex-girlfriend was in on the plot. How could she do that to me, and why?

Perhaps more concerning than the Covey is what they killed me to get. I'm the new owner of an antique Spanish powder horn, and the five-hundred-year-old wraith that resides within. His magic is ancient, and the only thing scarier than possessing his power is letting the bad guys get ahold of it.

Which brings us to now...

BLACK MAGIC OUTLAW

Chapter 1

My kingdom for one night of sleep.

A hideaway tucked into the Everglades isn't much of a kingdom, really, but it's what I had. An abandoned boathouse with a high corrugated ceiling and boarded up windows and doors, sans amenities like electricity or air conditioning, unless you count the airholes in the roof. Because of those, my bedroll's fitted into the one corner that stays dry when the Miami rains come. It was only drizzling now, but on the thin metal ceiling, it was enough to sound like the drum section of a parade.

Radiating outward from my bed were any number of crumpled Taco Bell wrappers. Abominations, every single one of them, but supremely delicious. I made no apologies for the mess. It was my home now. A reality. A necessity. So I stared at my rusty ceiling, in the darkness, wondering why I deserved such an exciting life that I couldn't manage some simple shut-eye.

Life on the lam looks sexy in the movies, in two-hour

cuts, but I was living it 24/7.

Cisco Suarez the shadow witch. The necromancer. The black magic outlaw. Man, those labels sound real neat. The problem is, I'm not the bad guy those monikers make me out to be. And there's nothing romantic about sleeping on the cold, wet floor.

There are some perks to the whole black magic angle, of course. Animists like me can channel spirit energy to our benefit. For example, right now Opiyel, my patron, was enabling me to see in the dark.

That was a good thing out here in the wild. People hear the Everglades and think, holy jeez, alligators, amirite? Believe you me, those little pansies are nothing to worry about. It's the spiders you need to look out for. Thus far my boathouse was arachnid free. That should've been enough to ease my mind and put me to sleep, but if I relaxed who'd keep an eye out for the spiders?

I passed the time by admiring a loose photo of my ex-girlfriend, elegant eyes half hidden by blonde hair. Trust me, being dead for ten years will do a number on any budding romance, but ours was something special. Emily and I have a love/hate relationship. Or more like a pretended-to-love-me/secretly-conspired-to-have-me-killed relationship. Love/hate's less wordy.

The point is, everything I knew was upside down. Returning from the dead, much like being an outlaw, isn't everything it's cracked up to be. But with the pain, at least I knew I was still human.

Jeez, the infamous outlaw Cisco Suarez was feeling

butthurt and staring at a picture of his college sweetheart. If I had a radio I'd play a Morrissey album or something. Thankfully, my little pity party was interrupted.

A croak scratched the back of my mind. I reached for the silver whistle beside my bed. It's my fetish. Silver's important to necromancy and it helps me listen to the shadows. One of my Cuban tree frogs had something to report.

I'd been stuck in this spot for a few weeks, so I'd done my best to build a small contingent of thralls. You might call them zombies. I kept several frogs: Kermit, Dig'em, Michigan J. I was already on Kermit Number IV because the local gators and snakes didn't have refined palettes. They'd gobble my little guys up, alive or dead. Guess times were tight in the Glades.

I sighed and closed my eyes to see through Kermie's, expecting the gaping maw of a predator enjoying a snack.

Flashlights. Bulletproof vests. Men wearing black march along the swamp in silence.

I sat up.

Four, six, seven men. SWAT gear, except the backs of their vests say—

The DROP team. Looks like the police finally found me.

Can't a guy get a break? You nearly burn down City Hall and turn a politician's front yard into the Thunderdome and all of a sudden you're Public Enemy Number One.

I rolled off the padding and slipped on my jeans and red alligator boots. My white tank top was already on. I hung the black twine and attached whistle around my neck and strapped my belt on, complete with giant skull-and-pentacle belt buckle and nylon belt pouch full of useful tokens for black magic. Lastly, since I go above and beyond the bare minimum of flair, I wrapped a black-leather spiked dog collar around my right forearm.

Most wizards have robes or long coats, but I'm not most wizards.

I turned to the single metal shelf against the wall. Jars of dirt, powder, and dried animal skin rested next to a bona fide set of metal vampire teeth and an enchanted burlap breathing mask. I had mundane stuff too. An old family album where I'd found Emily's picture. A toothbrush. I had stuff, is my point, and I didn't have the time or means to take it all.

My eyes fell to the reinforced lead safe in the corner. You couldn't see it through the closed door, but a single item was nestled inside: an antique bull powder horn with gold plating and Taíno pictographs. The Horn of Subjugation. In case it isn't obvious by the name, it's a spooky necromantic artifact.

"Wake up, Spaniard. We've got company."

Two orbs of red, like stoplights, burned into existence and focused on me. Around the eyes, a skull materialized. Then the rest of the body. A feathered helmet and breastplate. Pantaloons. A rapier and a flintlock hanging on a belt. Meet my tenuous ally: the ghost of a long-dead conquistador trapped in the Horn. A wraith.

"I thought you said this place was safe," he rasped.

I grimaced. I always did when I saw the Spaniard. His

stockings were torn and he wore fingerless gloves. It would've been better if his entire body was bone but sickly green patches of flesh wrapped his arms and legs. In my line of work I was used to seeing unnatural death, but this guy took the cake.

"What can I say?" I muttered, stuffing cash and a burner phone in my pockets. "The police found me."

The wraith didn't have eyebrows but he seemed to raise one. "The authorities. Humans. Any occultists among them?"

I shook my head. "Not an animist in the lot. Just semi-automatic rifles."

"What's the problem then? You are well equipped to dispatch them."

"The problem," I said, hoping this time the apparition would hear me, "is that I operate with a different set of morals than you do. I'm a good guy. The cops outside are good guys. I won't kill them."

He crossed his arms. "But *they'll* kill *you*."

"Yeah, well, they don't know any better."

The situation did seem kinda unfair, but I wouldn't give the wraith the satisfaction. In life he was in an army of conquerors, subjugating the native Arawak people of the Caribbean. As far as I knew, the Spaniard had practiced his black arts on Taíno slaves. His attempts at mastering death went swimmingly until the local shamans ensorcelled him into his powder horn and sealed it with enchanted gold.

That's a long way of saying I couldn't trust the wraith a whole lot. But he had helped me through my recent troubles and pledged to help me further. In my book, actions speak louder than horrifically skeletal appearances, and the Spaniard had been straight with me so far.

The apparition watched me study the safe the Horn was locked in. "Have you found the key?"

The key.

After some recent (and heavier than usual) poltergeist activity, I'd found the lead safe in a junkyard. I was operating on limited information at the time and thought the Horn was the cause of my problems. Maybe it was partially to blame, but that's neither here nor there. I'd hoped the lead lining would block any spirits from getting out.

If it was a deterrent, the Spaniard hadn't gotten the memo.

Even with the safe useless, it was the most secure place in my hideaway. I couldn't exactly keep an antiquated object of evil on my display shelf. Only, in the last week or so, I seemed to have misplaced the key. So now the police were bearing down on me, and I was stuck because I couldn't spirit away the artifact.

"If you will not kill them, you must run."

I gritted my teeth. "I can't hand you over to them."

The wraith shrugged. "I can deal with them, if you allow it."

"That's no better than me doing it myself. No hurting cops," I stressed. Seriously, the older you get, the more set in your ways you are. Imagine how hard it is to change the mind of a five-hundred-year-old necromancer.

An emotionless sigh escaped the apparition's ivory jaw. "Very well, brujo. If you like, I can cloud the minds of the mortals instead."

"A glamour?"

"More like a suggestion."

I frowned. Subjugation. I'd seen something of the wraith's power over the mind before, when he'd made a two-bit santero shoot himself in the head. I wondered just how powerful his manipulative magic was. It wasn't affecting me—at least I didn't think so. Generally, compulsions are more difficult on those familiar with spellcraft. But it didn't make me immune, either. I knew from horrible experience just how vulnerable I really was.

"Fine," I said. "But only enough so they don't notice us."

The Spaniard smiled. "I will merely block the scene from their minds. They will see the dank boathouse interior, but your possessions will be so unnoteworthy as to be invisible."

I nodded.

"There are two complications," he noted.

I double-checked Kermie's sight. The combat-ready police were swiftly moving down the swamp path. They'd be inside within a minute.

"Hurry."

The wraith tilted his head. "I am ready, but I cannot mask your presence. A living being, the object of their desire —it is too much."

Normally I could disappear into the shadows. It was kinda my thing. In this case, it was risky. My hiding spot would last only as long as the shadow remained, and every single DROP team officer had high-powered LED flashlights affixed to their guns.

I glanced at the doors. The near one that faced the path (and approaching police) was boarded over. Several metal roll-up doors that opened to the concrete boat platform were currently shut tight. Opening them would be loud. There was one more door, identical to the first, at the far end of the boathouse. I'd be headed that way anyway, deeper into the Everglades.

I started to the rear of the building. "I'll be back when it's over," I told him.

My companion raised his hand for me to stop. "It's not so simple, brujo. While I am bound to the Horn, my magicks require the presence of another occultist."

I twisted my lips, hearing this information for the first time. "You can't act without me?"

"In the sense you speak of, no."

I was starting to understand why so many people wanted the Horn.

Twenty seconds till entry.

"Screw that, *amigo*. I'm not signing my soul away today."

"My requirements are less dramatic than that. I merely need you to be close at hand and willful of the suggestion."

His words chilled me. If his power indeed couldn't have been used without my consent, however implicit, then that meant I had wanted that santero to die.

"Once the working has started," continued the Spaniard, "I can manage without you."

I opened my mouth to tell him I'd changed my mind, but

the sound of boots sloshing in mud ended the conversation. I moved away from the doorway, deeper into the large room.

The boathouse has a high ceiling that overhangs the front of the building, sort of like a covered porch where the boats roll out to. Although the building is mostly shielded from the rain, a couple areas of the overhang are exposed to the outside where the wall is broken away. Access is as simple as getting on the rafters that crisscross overhead. Not as far as the ceiling but still unreachable.

I leapt as high as I could and reached out for the wood beam. A coil of shadow unfurled from the ceiling and snaked around my wrist, yanking me several feet higher until my arms found purchase. As far as shadow magic goes, that was a gimme.

Something slammed into the barricaded front door. It smashed open violently, but only a crack. That's why it was barricaded. Strangely, there wasn't a follow-up strike. Everything went completely silent except for a single toiling sound, like a coin rolling on the concrete. My confusion turned to shock when the entire boathouse exploded in a brilliant flash of white.

Chapter 2

A flashbang. Step one of breaching a building. My grip on the rafter loosened as a shockwave battered against me. I reflexively snapped my eyes shut and turned away from the light. Legs dangling, I heaved myself onto the beam just in time to hear wood splintering below. Those were the door supports, still hanging tough.

My eyes burned. The spellcraft that gifted me with shadow sight made my retinas especially sensitive to light. I blinked away the charm, black tears falling from my eyes and restoring them to their normal green color, but when I forced my eyes open I couldn't see anything but white. For the moment, I was blind.

The pounding on the door below culminated in a loud crash, followed by debris skidding along the concrete floor. Booted footsteps marched over what was left of the makeshift barricade that secured me from the wilderness. So much for keeping the spiders out. And I had just fixed that door after a zombie high priest knocked it off its hinges.

The life of an outlaw animist.

I was above eye level and in complete darkness, but still in an exposed position. I slid along the rafter, still blind, hoping to hit the wall before being noticed. I guess it was finally time for something to go my way because I found safety before being brushed with an errant beam of light (or bullet). I nestled snugly into the overhang, resting on the wooden beam, careful not to make a noise by touching the corrugated metal, and drew the shadow over me.

"Clear," came a voice from the front door.

"Clear," answered another officer from the back.

Two brilliant flares pulsed through my already-white vision and I ducked low. They were looking around with their flashlights. At least my sight was returning.

"He's not here," complained one of the men.

"Keep your guard up," ordered another. "Double-check the shadows."

I recognized the voice with the good ideas because he was a friend of mine. Did I not mention that my best friend, Evan Cross, commands the DROP team?

Evan knows I'm an animist. He has ever since high school, when he was the blond-haired star quarterback of the football team and I was that weird kid that played with dead things. He's seen me dabble but doesn't trust black magic. Maybe he's the smart one. Ten years ago, I discovered the Horn of Subjugation. Soon after, a sect of creatures calling themselves the Covey killed me and my family. That's a pretty solid I-told-you-so.

Except, for some reason, I came back. A few weeks ago I

woke up in a dumpster in South Beach. Muscles, tattoos, the works. I found out I was a super-powered zombie hit man during my absence. Besides killing the vampire who'd murdered me, I crossed paths with the rest of the Covey as well as one corrupt politician—the city commissioner who happens to be Evan's boss.

So my buddy's in a bind. He totally means well, but he's compromised. Working for my enemies, lecturing me like some self-righteous hard-ass. Admittedly, I don't adhere to the most legal of operating practices, but don't take his side. I may have decked Evan but he shot me. And did I mention he married my ex-girlfriend, Emily? With best friends like him, who needs enemies?

The rest of the DROP team was a different story. I'd never shared beers with them or congratulated their graduating the police academy. The only time they'd ever seen me was a recent confrontation that turned into the scene of a ghost movie. The DROP team saw some things they probably shouldn't have that night. One of their own died. I bet each and every one of them had recurring nightmares. More to the point, each one personally blamed me.

Evan might have a soft spot for old Cisco Suarez, but everyone else on the team wanted blood.

As my eyes adjusted to the darkness, I saw them up close and personal for the first time.

"This is a wild goose chase," grumbled a squat officer. He was bald but young, with hard eyes.

"Keep it contained, Sergeant," said Evan, pacing to my

sleeping corner.

He kicked a fast-food wrapper and shined a flashlight at the lead safe and the metal shelf. It didn't do a whole lot of good. He turned away as if he'd just inspected a blank wall. The wraith's magic was impressive; mine would've failed there.

"I want men searching the perimeter," ordered Evan.

The sergeant clicked his teeth. "He's not here, Lieutenant."

"I know that. I want to check for evidence that he ever *was* here. Our target's been in the wind for two weeks. We need to narrow down his whereabouts." Evan looked past his grumpy sergeant to a skinny detective. "Check the perimeter, Mullen."

"Yes, sir," came the voice. Mullen marched outside with some others, leaving the two alone.

They looked around in silence for a few minutes. Then the sergeant chuckled coarsely and shook his head. "Maybe this Cisco character was never here at all."

From a few feet away, Evan shifted his flashlight beam to his subordinate's face. "What are you trying to say, Sergeant?"

A smile. "Nothing."

"No, Garcia, I'm not letting you off the hook that easily. I want to know what you meant by that."

The sergeant's face tightened and he pushed Evan's flashlight away. "Fine," he grumbled. "It's just that some of the guys are talking. They think maybe you have a connection to this guy. That you're protecting him." Look who had the good ideas now.

Evan's cold eyes burned. "Is it *some guys* talking or *you*?"

Garcia shrugged.

My friend snorted. "You keep shoveling that BS, Garcia. You want command of the DROP team? Do it based on merit instead of mudslinging. We're all after the same thing here. I have the same intel as you. The local gangs had dealings with someone named Cisco two weeks ago, but all contact was since cut off. A known accomplice, now missing, had once used this site."

Missing. I guess that was the official story they were going with on paper. The vampire was dead in reality. Those were his metal teeth on my shelf.

I eavesdropped intently. Evan was doing what I expected. After all, he couldn't readily admit that his old buddy Cisco was back from the dead, determined to kill anyone with a hand in his murder. Besides a first name, no one knew who I really was except for Evan and the supernatural bastards I wanted to kill. That worked in my favor because they couldn't come right out and reveal my identity without risking exposure. Besides, my ID wouldn't help anybody. It's not like I have an address of record, unless you count Saint Martin's Cemetery.

The real problem was that Evan constantly second-guessed my motives, just as I did his. My ex, Emily, had worked with the Covey. Now she was Evan's wife. I was sure Evan didn't know the truth back then, but I would kill to read his mind now. Where did his loyalties lie?

I guess I'd gotten my answer as soon as he barged into

my Everglades hideaway.

Sergeant Garcia scoffed. "You're one to talk about merit. You were gifted this job through your wife's connections. Except I hear Commissioner Alvarez isn't too happy with you these days. It's only a matter of time before you're back in uniform at Central Station."

Evan clenched his jaw and stepped right into the shorter man's personal space. Before he could get a word out, the skinny detective returned.

"Nothing outside, sir. It's just wilderness. No signs of a camp or hunting or anything. Maybe we should call Fish and Wildlife?"

Evan winced. "Don't bother. FWC won't find anything." He glared at Sergeant Garcia. "We have other possible locations and we're going to check each one to rule them out. Cisco's in Miami, and we're going to find him."

Evan Cross stormed to the doorway. Garcia shrugged with a smile, and ran his flashlight over the rafters. I shied away as light washed over me. The shadow could only help so much. I ducked onto the overhang and my alligator boot slipped and echoed against the metal.

The beam of light froze. Evan's came back on and pointed my way, soon joined by Mullen's.

"What was that?" asked Garcia.

"An animal?" suggested Mullen.

I pressed myself down on the corrugated metal eave overhanging the boat platform. The weight made the rotted support beam give way. A steel brace broke free and the entire panel, with me on it, bent and clattered to the cement floor outside the front of the boathouse. A monster truck crash would've made less noise.

Smooth. From eavesdropping to eave dropping. I was on a roll.

Chapter 3

"Someone's there!" yelled Evan, mobilizing his troops.

At the moment, there was a wall dividing me from said troops. Although it had several roll-up doors, they were locked. Evan and the others would run around through the front door, only set back by several seconds.

The cops already outside were a more immediate problem, but I didn't see any on the boat platform. I spun, considering my options. Time was quickly running out. Without really thinking, I made a beeline for the edge of the platform and bounded into the swamp. I splashed down just as the DROP team rounded the corner.

"It's in the water!"

"What is it?"

I kicked my feet and went deeper, thankful the moon wasn't bright tonight. Flashlight beams broke the water. I put the silver whistle to my lips and blew some air into it that bubbled past me. I hoped it would work.

I checked another tree frog's vision. The cops were

outside, guns drawn, facing the swamp. They knew something had been in the rafters and jumped in the swamp, but they didn't know what. With any luck they would chalk it up to Everglades creepiness.

I swam further away from their search, kicking up mud from the swamp floor. My chest grew tight. I had to surface. Luckily I found a thick patch of saw grass to come up behind. They don't call it the River of Grass for nothing.

"That was not a damn bird," swore Garcia, after I could hear them again. "It went into the water." Several DROP team officers swept their gazes over the surface of the swamp.

"He's right," said Evan grudgingly. "It was big. We can search the swamp if we need to." Evan pulled a radio to his lips. "Miami, you there?"

The speaker buzzed back. A female dispatcher spoke out individual letters. "QSL." Miami Q codes.

"This is DROP 1. Does SRT have an airboat unit on standby?" asked Evan.

"QRX, DROP 1."

I grimaced. If the cops got an airboat out here, I could never outrun them.

"Hold it," called out Garcia. He pointed to the center of the swamp. A fifteen-foot alligator surfaced and floated lazily past them.

Two of the detectives recoiled from the water. Mullen raised his rifle.

"It was a gator," said the sergeant.

Evan's forehead knotted. "In the rafters?"

The cops turned and examined the roof of the boathouse. The panel I'd jarred loose was still half attached with its other end touching the cement floor. It was basically a ramp to the roof now.

"Was this overhang like that before?" asked Mullen. An officer shrugged.

Meanwhile, the alligator drifted away from them and towards my spot in the grass.

Evan scratched his head and spoke into the radio. "Miami? 0-7 that airboat request. We're not gonna need it."

"QSL, DROP 1," came the answer as he clipped the radio back to his vest.

"Now I've seen everything," laughed Garcia nervously. He lowered his weapon. "Look how big that thing is."

He wasn't kidding. Fifteen feet of leathery hide, all swimming my way. The police abandoned their search of the swamp, choosing instead to focus on the alligator. It would be difficult to make a move with them watching.

I waited, as still as the unrippled surface of the water. The black creature neared. Its eyes were dark orbs on a barren island. As the gator reached my patch of grass, he lifted his head and revealed a long set of dirty teeth.

I calmly checked the boathouse. Garcia was still watching, but it couldn't be helped. I had to chance it. With a deep breath, I slipped beneath the water. The alligator passed and I reached underneath and grabbed his front leg. Once I was hitched, the gator kicked ahead and swam into the darkness.

Yes, I had an alligator zombie too. Admittedly not the

cuddliest pet, but you can't blame me. I'd been in the Everglades for weeks without TV or internet. I couldn't afford to be choosy with my hobbies.

I held my breath as long as I could before bringing my face up for air alongside the alligator's thick body. It was a good angle that hid me from distant onlookers. Not a lot of people know this—hell, I didn't know it until my stint in the Glades—but gators can work up a good clip in the water, something approaching twenty miles per hour. I was one Mr. Toad's Wild Ride away from safety. (No, I didn't name my gator Mr. Toad, although now that I think of it, I wish I did. His actual moniker? Leatherhead. Am I a product of the TV generation or what?)

In no time my chauffeur got me to an embankment far from the action. I scrambled past the mud and did my best to empty my boots, but the grime was staying with me for a while. I tossed my water-logged cell phone into the water and was just coming to terms with my predicament when Leatherhead jerked his head around.

A stray black cat hopped through tall grass and glanced my way with bright green eyes. The gator took a step toward it.

"Not this time," I commanded. "Go distract the boys at the boathouse."

Leatherhead waddled off silently. If he hadn't been a zombie I would've sworn he was disappointed.

I wasn't partial to feeding cats to gators. This cat, specifically, was special. He was one of my thralls, another zombie, except I'd lost my connection with him many miles and a couple weeks back.

"Come here, boy."

The black cat blinked bored eyes at me.

I put my whistle to my lips, blew the water out, and called the cat with a silent chime. It turned away, waved an angry tail at me, and jumped into the brush. Cats.

"Bad zombie," I grumbled.

I took careful steps after him, wondering what the hell was up. Believe it or not, despite my current accommodations, I'm not much of an outdoorsman. Navigating through wetlands in the middle of the night wasn't my idea of fun.

"Is someone out there?" came a crisp voice. I ducked into the grass. Another flashlight. Another officer. His radio chirped and he called for backup.

What was the DROP team still checking the perimeter for?

"City of Miami Police," he announced. "If someone's out there, identify yourself."

I frowned. I wasn't Cisco Suarez, I was a snake. A gator. A woodland creature. I just needed to stay low and he'd give up his search.

The cat made a hacking sound, like a bark mixed with a growl. The officer swept his beam of light across the tall grass. The cat's eyes flashed yellow as the light hit them.

He was staring at me. He wanted to show me something.

I waited till the flashlight scanned another area and crawled ahead. I shoved and shook the tall grass, but it couldn't be helped. Either I moved or I was a sitting duck.

Like a cartoon prison fugitive, I froze when the light washed over me and continued moving while in darkness. All I needed was a black-and-white striped suit.

"You sure you see someone?" asked another officer from a distance. "We have lots of wildlife in the area. The lieutenant says we should pull back inside."

The other officer, much closer to me: "They don't got wolves out here, do they?"

A beat. "Panthers, I think."

The officer paused again. I didn't. I continued rustling ahead. I chased the cat to a tree, broke free of the grass, and kneeled in a circle of dirt. The cat was gone.

"Over there, I think," the officer said.

At the base of the tree was a ditch framed by two large roots. A den of sorts.

"You've got to be kidding," I muttered. "He went all Peter Rabbit on me."

The boot steps approached from behind. I checked around for the cat, but I knew where it had gone. With an exhausted sigh, I slipped into the hole in the ground, hoping there was a nook of shadow to hide in that the flashlight couldn't reach.

There was a nook all right.

Chapter 4

When you slip into an animal den, there are lots of things that can surprise you. Teeth, claws, venom—a hibernating bear. What I didn't expect was for the ground to give out. One second I was squeezing into a claustrophobic ditch, the next I was in free fall.

I tumbled head over heels for a prolonged second before my back thudded against solid ground. As your animist tour guide, I immediately figured where I was. It's just that I hadn't seen anything like it in quite a while. I guess, considering my ten-year sabbatical, there were a lot of things I hadn't seen for a while.

I was in a cavern of sorts. Something that would be real cozy with the mole people. Wide walls of bored dirt formed a large room with two exit passages leading away from each other at an angle. The ceiling was hardened dirt as well, with roots dangling in the air like claws. Behind me, the soil ramped up to a small entry filled with blinding light.

This wasn't the normal under-earth. Dig ten feet deep

anywhere in Miami and you'll find water, especially in the Everglades. This earth was lower than that. Only accessible by magic. In outdated legends, this was where magic came from.

You and I know that to be inaccurate, but it didn't make the place any less mysterious. I now sat in the Nether, what many call the underworld.

It's not damnation. It's not the shadow world, full of spirits of the dead, or anything like that. It's more like a lateral realm. Just another place, except this one ain't on Google Maps. The Nether isn't really in the same space as everything else, but if you know a bit of spellcraft (or happen to get inordinately lucky) you can find the nooks and crannies that lead here. What I found is called a rabbit hole by people in the know (like yours truly).

For perspective, it's important to realize that The World We Know is divided into steppes. The Earthly Steppe is Miami, North America, China, the planets, and the deepest reaches of space. What we call the universe. But there's another steppe below us: the Nether, land of the silvans. There are other types of Nether creatures, too—fiends, giants, scourgelings. They're sometimes collectively known as the fae or the wild folk, but the others aren't important. The true players down here are the silvans.

Humans aren't inherently magical. The few animists among us require spirits to channel magic. Nether beings, however, are born of it. They don't cast spells so much as utilize natural defense mechanisms. It's literally instinct with them. The West African vampire that killed me a decade ago, whose metal teeth rested on a shelf in my hideaway? He had been a Nether fiend.

So it's safe to say I was a wee bit nervous at having already drawn the attention of two of the fabled creatures. They stood over me with perplexed expressions, making me feel like a medical school cadaver.

Call me a pig, but the girl drew my eye first. It wasn't my fault, really, on account of her slight dress. What amounted to a sash of red cloth wrapped her small chest between her bare shoulders and midriff. Her impossibly skinny waist was well-muscled and transitioned into a shag of bona fide horse legs, complete with straight tail and white hooves.

She was a satyr, supple and feminine on top, yet powerful underneath.

She was pretty, too. Large doe eyes on a childlike face. Expressive eyebrows and flowing black hair that curled across her slender shoulders and back. I'd feel remiss if I failed to mention the flesh-toned horse ears that flopped down either side of her face, each with a large gold hoop earring. She wore only the bright red sash and a matching wrap around her waist.

Her companion was her polar opposite, and don't assume because I mentioned her first that he blended into the background, because he didn't. Like, not at all. He was huge, imposing, and—there's no gentle way to say this—a minotaur. That meant he had a full-on bull's head, ears twice as long as the satyr's (with twice as many earrings), thick brown horns planted in his skull (more earrings somehow), and a red Mohawk and chin-beard. And man, gold hoops must be the height of silvan fashion because he had a huge one that put all the others to shame dangling from his nostrils.

The minotaur's body was covered in a sheen of short brown fur, thinned over the chest and stomach to show off more muscles than I could count. He only wore a shoulder strap and simple leather breeches that cut out under his knees to reveal thick legs ending in black hooves.

As I studied him, he made a throaty grumble that vibrated his cheeks.

"Uh..." I started meekly, "you kind folks didn't happen to see my cat, did you?"

The minotaur's grumble ended in a sharp snort that shook the ring in his nose. "A human," he growled, considering the situation. "I *hate* humans."

"If it's any consolation, I'm with you on hating a fair share of humans too."

Another rumble-snort. The minotaur turned to the satyr. "We should kill him."

Sheesh. That's silvans for you.

Everybody knows what silvans are. Not always by name, but we've all seen the artwork. We've all heard the legends. There once was a time way back that silvans interacted with humans openly. Greek scholars debated their nature. Sages sought out their advice. It wasn't until the Middle Ages that human technology became a real threat to them. Mass warfare, the end of paganism, it caused the silvans to lie low and all but disappear.

So yeah, maybe a little bad blood between the races. But,

to be fair, they have their own perfectly good steppe called the Nether. You don't see too many humans foraging down here on their turf. Present company excluded.

I watched the satyr hopefully. Tried to find sympathy in her light-brown eyes. Some common ground, maybe.

You're not supposed to trust silvans, you know, but satyrs are generally good-natured. Throughout history they've often brought luck upon mankind. I could use some of that.

"I really don't think I'm worth killing," I chanced. "Just a human, and all that." I waited for her verdict.

Her brown eyes pinched closed in mirth. The satyr opened her mouth and... giggled.

Not exactly the vote of confidence I was hoping for.

The minotaur grunted and his jowls settled into a smile. Then he reached over his shoulder and drew a kukri from a sheath on his back. At least now I knew what the leather shoulder strap was for. Just my luck it was a giant knife with a bent blade.

Chapter 5

Kukris are mean-looking short swords that sport a sharp angle in the middle of the blade. The inward bend makes it more of a raking weapon, imposing leverage in close quarters. Good for tunnels, I figured. The minotaur jabbed it in my general direction.

Whether it was a strike or a warning, I didn't hesitate to phase into the darkness. There are lots of problems with the Nether, but no one will ever tell you it isn't well shadowed. Even next to a rabbit hole, I had good coverage down here. My body backed into the ground, slipped into the darkness, and slid forward, between the two silvans.

This kind of dash only works for short distances. A few yards, maybe more with a long shadow. The good thing is, when you're talking giant knives, sometimes a couple inches is all the difference between life and death.

I materialized behind the wild folk before they caught on to what had happened. Taking advantage of their confusion, I drew a line from the shadow, a tight cord of ether that wrapped around the minotaur's blade like a whip. My hand with the dog-collar bracelet—my fetish to Opiyel, the Shadow Dog—closed into a fist and wrenched to the side. The shadow whip mimicked the motion, tugging hard at the kukri.

It was a great move. Perfectly executed. Lesser foes would've been disarmed, but the minotaur's grip held firm against my attempt. The large knife remained in his hands.

I yanked on the shadow twice more, but the beast was strong. He wrapped his other hand around the blade's handle and turned to face me with a rumbling growl.

"A wizard," he spat, ear flicking in contempt. "I *hate* wizards."

This guy.

"Actually," I said, carefully keeping my shadow whip in place. "Most people call me witch or necromancer or even brujo. Wizard is a bit too *Harry Potter* for me."

Another giggle from the satyr. I wondered if she got the reference.

"Release my weapon," commanded the minotaur, tugging at it.

His strength was impressive. It took noticeable effort to keep the shadow on the blade. What the minotaur didn't know was that my spellcraft couldn't wield the knife like some kind of ghostly soldier. It could only pull at it. If the silvan just released it, the pretentious sword would clatter to the floor. Worse then, this would turn into a grappling match. Never grapple with a minotaur.

"Throok," chimed the satyr.

Us guys tugged at the knife, ignoring her, eyes locked in an impromptu staring contest. Sure he was seven feet tall and put my ample muscles to shame but, damn it, I would beat him if he just blinked.

"Throok," repeated the girl.

The minotaur spun around and the line of shadow wrapped across his back, as if he could use leverage to free it. Maybe he could. I strained against his power. Cutting and running back up the rabbit hole was starting to sound awfully good. You might think the DROP team was a headache, but you've never dealt with silvans before.

The satyr balled her hands into fists and stomped on the floor. "THROOK!" she screamed.

The minotaur and I finally turned to her.

"What the crap is a throok?" I prodded.

The minotaur grumbled, and the satyr composed herself and smiled. "Not a *what*, wizard. A *who*. Throok is my bodyguard."

My eyes wandered to the seven-foot-tall steroid machine. "You're Throok?"

I blinked. Damn.

"Put your kukri away, Throok," she said.

His muscles remained tense. "He's seen you. That information is valuable."

I knotted my brow. "To who? I wouldn't know who to ask or what to say."

Believe me, the last thing I wanted was to get involved in silvan politics. The various circles perpetuate endless feuds and plots against each other. Besides, silvans don't really have currency. They trade and barter. Sure, they might hoard the occasional treasure, but they usually deal in favors.

"We can use him," she said. "He's talented."

"He's dangerous," answered Throok.

"If he weren't he wouldn't be useful."

The minotaur grumbled. He did that a lot.

"Guys," I said, relaxing my stance, "would you quit talking about me like I wasn't here?"

The satyr girl smiled and rested delicate fingers on Throok's arm. "Sheathe your blade."

He frowned and turned to me. "Release my weapon."

"You won't attack me?"

"I swear it. Not until it is again unsheathed."

I was floored by his generous pledge. That bought me, what, three seconds of life? Still, looking into the satyr's large eyes, I thought I'd found my common ground. I opened my fist and the shadow dissolved.

Throok regained his balance and hooked the blade over his back. I stayed ready, expecting him to immediately unsheathe it, but his hand came away empty.

The satyr smiled and patted his arm. "That wasn't so bad," she consoled, hopping over to me. She put a dainty hand on my shoulder, leaned close, and winked. "You see?"

I tried not to flinch away from the silvan. She looked real cute (besides the half-horse thing) but that didn't mean she was innocent. The wild folk are famed tricksters but, again, I was relying on the age-old wisdom that satyrs were benevolent.

"My name's Ceela," she said. She did this cute thing where her nose wiggled when she said her name. Adorable.

The minotaur grunted.

Okay, Cisco, stay focused. I didn't want to be known as the famous outlaw who fell victim to a wink.

"What brings you here?" asked Ceela.

I shrugged. "Why? This your land?"

She giggled. "The Margins of the Nether are owned by no one, and there are plenty more wild lands still. No, our dominion is much deeper."

I nodded. Any portions of the Nether that connected to the Earthly Steppe were easily susceptible to outside invasion. Not the most stable place to set up a homestead, but it was all I'd ever seen of the realm.

"He's running," observed the minotaur. "Out of breath, soaking wet. He brings trouble."

Ceela's eyes widened in fascination. "Is this true?"

"Hardly," I said. "Cisco Suarez doesn't run. He merely *avoids* when convenient." She raised an eyebrow. Glad I was so amusing. "I don't want to hurt the police," I added.

Throok brought his head back. "An outlaw."

"In the technical sense, sure, but it's more of a flashy title. The important thing is the police officers aren't animists and they can't enter the Nether. They'll be gone in a jiffy."

Ceela hummed a singsong melody and strolled around me before coming full circle back to her bodyguard. "What do we care for the justice of Earthly authorities? You can stay in our hole."

"I thought you said it wasn't yours."

She hunched her slender shoulders and I thought her sash would fall off. She was so skinny I wondered what kept it on. I didn't see a tie in the back or anything. Of course, only real clothes needed such trappings. Silvans could shift their appearance slightly with magic. They couldn't exactly alter their features willy-nilly, but they could change their dress and appear more human at times. I wondered if her meager clothes were some kind of illusion.

No, if it was spellcraft that implied it could be dispelled. This was innate magic. A glamour. Probably as automatic to them as breathing.

"This place is not ours," amended Ceela. "I merely mean to say you can pass freely as you will."

I nodded. "Good to hear 'cause I was thinking I'd take off." I stepped toward the bright light of the rabbit hole.

"Wait," rushed the satyr. "Sit. Stay a while."

Throok cleared his throat. "We do not have time for this, Ceela."

She waved him off. "Don't you see? We can help each other."

"Whoa," I cut in. "Let's get something straight. I don't need your help. I only came down here by accident and it's already getting claustrophobic in here, but maybe that's on account of the seven-foot-tall bull-man."

Throok considered reaching for his knife. Ceela waved him off.

"You can slip away," she said. "I don't doubt that much after seeing your magic with my two eyes. But what happens the next time your authorities come knocking? They won't likely forget about you, will they? What's to stop them from knocking tomorrow night? Or the next?" She leaned into me again and did that nose-wiggle thing. Really playing up the cute angle. "I can make them forget your place forever."

I took a step back. Human interaction with silvans is the stuff of history, much of it clouded by legend, so it's hard to know definitively what they're capable of. The last thing I wanted to do was endanger the police officers, but if they could just... forget? Things would be safer for everyone.

"You won't hurt them?"

"We know better than to harm humans in their steppe."

"You've never been to their steppe," corrected the minotaur.

She rolled her eyes. "Maybe I keep secrets even from you, Throok."

He scoffed. "It's goes against the Table of Oak to mingle with humans before your seventeenth name day."

"Before your—" I dropped my jaw. "What are you, sixteen? You're not even old enough to..."

She winked at me.

"Drink," I finished. I turned to Throok. "What about you?"

He raised his head high. "I am a full adult. Seventeen."

I slapped my hand to my forehead. "Look, I really wasn't expecting to babysit..."

"Don't ridicule us," said Ceela. "Silvans mature early and quickly. Many of us have full charges at seventeen, and many are married before even that."

"But you're just kids. I can't ask you to go out there and risk yourself for me."

Throok chuckled, but Ceela answered. "We were on our way to your steppe anyway when you interrupted us," she said. "We will appear human to your kind, if we allow them to see us at all."

I sighed. The offer was tempting and I was out of objections, but I knew there was a catch. "What do you want in return?"

"Simple," she chimed. "Pretend you never saw us. We weren't here."

"That's it?"

Throok grumbled but she ignored him.

"That's it. Sit tight and give us time to bedazzle your law enforcement above. We'll move on and disappear into the Everglades. You'll likely never see us again."

If only. How could I turn that down? "Fine," I said, relenting. "Deal."

She smiled and tapped me on the shoulder again. This time I did flinch. "Where is your home?" she asked.

"It's a boathouse. Just go up the swamp, halfway to the road. The police will be there, though."

She nodded like I had just asked her to pick up a Big Mac. "Your authorities will be no problem. They'll pack up and not think on your haven again."

She put her lips to her palm and blew a kiss my way. Throok growled under his breath, but she grabbed his arm and led him away. They took two steps up the rabbit hole before the light consumed them. I wondered if they'd tumble on their asses on the other side like I had.

With the silvans gone, I was alone in the cavern. It seemed spacious now, with a ceiling higher than Throok could reach. I wondered which of the two passages they had come from, which dominions lay which way. I didn't know much about silvan circles, but I knew enough that I didn't want to go exploring.

I sat on my haunches and frowned. Maybe the lack of sunlight was making me grumpy. Maybe Throok used to be a jovial fellow. What there were no maybes about was that something was wrong.

I'd surprised the silvans. One wanted me dead, the other wanted me alive. Throok was worried that I'd seen them. He was shocked that Ceela might've violated the Oak Table and visited the Earthly Steppe before, yet that's what they were about to do anyway. That meant they were up to something. Desperate times, perhaps. I suddenly got the feeling that I wasn't the only one running.

Something scratched my butt. I figured I was sitting on an ant trail or something. When I checked beneath me, a black spider skittered away.

I jumped, and I mean JUMPED. I hate spiders. Really hate them. In my book, nothing with more than four legs deserves to live, but I can give some things a pass. Ladybugs, octopuses, grasshoppers—they don't bother me. Then again, none of those things lay eggs in your eyeball while you sleep.

I scrambled to my feet and wiped my jeans. My tank top. I upended my boots and checked my socks. I was good. I could share an underground cavern with a single spider, right?

Except there were two spiders. And three when I really looked. They weren't giant anansi trickster spiders or anything (believe me, I've dealt with those). They were tiny, normal spiders. Sometimes those are the worst kind.

I backed up to the wall, wondering if I'd stayed in the Nether long enough for the silvans to do their thing. I should've left, but I didn't. When I glanced at the passageway and saw a lanky woman wearing a long, white gown, I knew I'd lost my chance.

Chapter 6

The woman clutched the edge of the hallway as if to hide around it. It was a useless gesture. She was thin, but there was simply no place to go.

I was pressed against the wall myself. I manifested enough courage to unglue my ass and did my best to ignore the spiders on the floor. My pained face must've been obvious because the woman in the white dress giggled. I was a regular comedy act down here.

I cleared my throat. "It's nothing," I said, trying to sound tough. "Don't be afraid. They're just spiders."

She didn't move and I figured it was me she was afraid of.

"I'm Cisco Suarez. What's your name?"

She blinked at me. "Are you lost?"

"I guess I am," I answered in a jovial tone. "You can come out. I won't hurt you."

She smiled but her eyes were still tense. I beckoned with my hand. She glanced behind her before easing away from the wall.

Her nightgown was a lot more formal than I'd expected from the Nether. It covered the length of her legs, only revealing bare feet when she stepped ahead. Her waist was wrapped in a corset which left her shoulders bare. Her arms were skinny and undernourished, and her face was one that could've been pretty but circumstance had made plain. Her long black hair was straight but tattered, thin as a thread. I couldn't put my finger on it. Something about this woman was sad.

"I get lost too, sometimes," she said. Her skin and dress were smudged with dirt. I couldn't blame her, down here. Hell, I'd just gone for a dip in a swamp.

"What about now?" I asked.

She looked over her shoulder again but didn't answer.

One of the spiders on the floor got too close and I kicked it away.

"Don't do that!" she exclaimed. She hurried forward on her haunches. The woman cupped her hands around the black spider and then produced it in her palm. I grimaced. "It's a living thing, with its own job to do."

Yeah, like freak me out. She must've seen my discomfort because she set it down at the edge of the cavern. "It's special in its own way. All of us are. Each with our own story."

I couldn't tell if that was an invitation to ask about hers. Can I read women or what?

She watched my befuddled expression and gathered the confidence to approach. She was tall. I mean, not Throok tall, but she met me eye to eye. I wondered if she was human. Slim odds, down here.

"You don't talk much," she deduced.

"I keep up an inner monologue."

She smiled and wiped dirt from her cheek. There were lines of grime under her short fingernails. The woman had the mannerisms of a child but, even though I couldn't place her age, was much older than that. As I considered her, we heard panting sounds coming from the passage and she glanced behind her.

What now?

"Grettle," came a nasally voice. A man appeared in the opening she'd come through, but he was anything but. He was a faun. Half goat, half man. This was beginning to feel like a chapter of *Alice in Wonderland*.

Shorter than the satyr, more hunched over, the faun's winding ram horns made up for his loss in stature. He had shaggy, brown goat-legs with cloven hooves, a bare torso except for tufts of hair on his shoulders and forearms, and wore a leather skirt and belt. You see what I mean about clothes in the Nether?

Unlike the satyr, the faun's face was less human. Not completely goatlike, but animalistic, with a flattened nose, orange eyes with those freaky goat pupils, and exposed fangs. He flicked his pointed ears when he saw me and stroked his goat beard. His other hand held what looked like a cross between a hatchet and a boomerang, carved out of bone.

"You can't run off like that, Grettle," he chided. The

faun approached us warily. He clamped a clawed hand around the woman's arm and pulled her away, never taking his eyes off me.

"Now wait just a minute," I said.

"For you?" he chortled. "Not a chance."

"Be nice, Orpheus," said Grettle.

Orpheus. Grettle. Ceela. Throok. Nether names.

Orpheus snorted, but it didn't carry the gravitas of the minotaur's. "You're a human, aren't you? What are you doing in the Margins?"

"I have my reasons."

He nodded absently, looking up the other passage and then considering the rabbit hole. "Where is she?"

I waited a beat. "Grettle?"

"Not her, human. The satyr. Where is the satyr?"

I scrunched my eyebrows. "Is this some kind of hypothetical riddle?"

"Never lie to a trickster, human. Fauns are the masters of lies. Are you alone down here?"

"Yes," I answered truthfully. "Just us and the spiders." Grettle smiled.

"Then we have you outnumbered," he taunted.

I didn't know if he meant the spiders or something else. I preferred the something else.

"Back away, Grettle," he said, shoving her toward the passage.

"But—"

"I said back away. I can handle the human."

I laughed. "You can *what*?"

The faun tapped his hatchet against his black hooves to shake dirt away. "This doesn't need to go bad for you, human."

"The name's Cisco."

He narrowed his eyes. "Just tell me where the satyr went and we'll leave you be."

"*We*," I repeated. "Is that word used differently in the Nether? Because topside it means more than one person."

Orpheus snorted again. "So be it." He threw the boomerang at me.

Chapter 7

The first thing I did was wonder: who uses boomerangs?

My second action was more pragmatic. I lunged to the side as the projectile spun past me. There was a heft to it, I could tell, because of the wind that buffeted me as it went by.

The faun leaned forward in anticipation. I hate to disappoint everyone, but I'm no amateur. I knew that boomerang was coming back around for me. I turned and flicked my hand at it, sending a twine of shadow to wrap it up.

The boomerang sliced right through my magic like butter. Maybe I'd be called the dairy witch from now on.

With only a second to spare, I phased into the darkness just as the projectile flew at me on its return trip. I was fast enough, but it still caught me. Instead of whiffing right through me, the boomerang rapped against my head, pulled me out of the shadow, and knocked me on my ass.

Orpheus caught the weapon with ease and chuckled. I pushed to my knees and faced him with a scowl. There were spiders all over the floor, but at least they were staying away from the big boys. A tickle in my hairline concerned me. I patted the dirt off my hands and rubbed my head just above the temple. It came away with blood.

"Had enough, human?" he taunted.

"You kidding? You don't win a fight with one lucky shot."

Orpheus relaxed his features. "This is what you call a fight topside?"

I did my best Throok impression and growled as I stood. I didn't have seven feet but I was a couple heads taller than this runt. When I came at him, though, he didn't look concerned.

Orpheus now held his weapon like a hatchet, swinging it in his hand. I feinted and stepped away, wary of diving back into the shadow. My guess was his weapon was enchanted. Strong enough magic could hit me when I hid in the darkness. In those situations, it was best not to hide.

I stepped into his next blow, raising my left arm as the hatchet crashed into it. Blue light flared, but the Norse protection tattoo along my forearm held stronger than full plate. I didn't feel a thing.

I had another tattoo on my palm that could manifest a shield of energy. That one was meant for small projectiles, like bullets. It wouldn't do jack against melee weapons, so I was stuck in hand-to-hand combat.

I punched Orpheus in the face with said hands. He recoiled in shock and I went for another. The faun lowered his winding horns, and the impact nearly broke my knuckles.

Orpheus rolled his weapon arm away from my armored arm. I devoted both hands to keeping the hatchet at bay, and that's when he hit me. A cloven hoof cracked into the side of my knee. I dropped halfway to the ground, to his height. Orpheus spun around, and this time the hoof barreled into my chest. I crashed to the floor again, hacking up spittle.

The short faun cracked his shoulders. "Another lucky shot, I suppose."

My leg hurt. If it wasn't for the magic fortifying my body, my knee would've shattered. This time when I stood, the sound I made was more of a grunt. Less anger, more pain.

The faun considered the rabbit hole. "It's against the Table for younglings to venture to the other steppes. She didn't go overground, did she?"

"Who?" They say a sucker's born every minute. Better than being a snitch, I suppose.

The boomerang flew at me again. I slipped into the shadow, but this time I used it for speed. I dashed to the side quicker than my body could've managed, escaping the path of the hurled weapon. I solidified in a crouch. The boomerang circled around and came back for me.

Instead of moving, I reached into the shadow on the floor. My hand pushed down, into the darkness, like the dirt was a liquid surface. When my hand emerged, it was wrapped around the sawed-off shotgun that I stored in the ether. It was an old piece, a breech-loading model with a single barrel, but I was a good shot. I raised the weapon, waited a beat for the boomerang to bear down on me, and fired. The birdshot erupted from the shotgun and sent the boomerang into the wall and clattering to the floor.

"Huh," said Orpheus with a scowl.

I smiled as I ejected the shell, reached into my belt pouch, and loaded another round. This one was an original creation I call fireshot: birdshot rounds opened up and modified with orange spark powder. You don't practice black magic in Miami without picking up some voodoo tricks. Shadow magic is good and all, but sometimes you need a bigger punch.

A sharp whistle escaped the faun's lips. I raised my sawed off at him, but little creatures flooded in from the passage before I could call him off. Little men, humanoid, shorter even than Orpheus. Three feet max. These bad boys had large heads, gray skin mottled with warts, and crooked, disjointed features. Patches of their withered skin were hairless; other sections that weren't meant for it were hairy: knuckles, elbows. They were clothed in rags and twigs and leaves and were generally disgusting. Awful thing to say about an entire race of creatures, but there it was. Their gray skin and yellow eyes tipped me off to what they were: spriggans.

Slaves and underlings to higher fae, spriggans weren't silvans themselves. They didn't resemble humans or animals —they were more like little goblins—and they were shit at magic. Not a single one of these ragged sleeves had a trick up it, but there were a lot of them. Ten, fifteen, and more streaming into the room. With those numbers, claws and teeth start becoming extremely tactical.

And unfortunately, my one-shot-at-a-time sawed off wasn't gonna cut it in these conditions.

As the room filled with the ugly fuckers, they proved me right. No formation, no talking—they just charged straight at me without pretense.

I fired my shotty at the nearest two. Half of one's head exploded and the other erupted in flames. The fire startled the horde and backed them away. I dropped the gun to the floor and it submerged in the shadow. Then I went into my pouch and retrieved a small sack of powder that I upturned into my open palm.

Powder might be a bad word. Bone dust is more accurate. Not just dust, either. You don't get access to industrial grinders in the boonies so the stuff was pretty chunky, like gravelly sand. Add the six intact water moccasin fangs and you can probably deduce how I came about the source material (and why I don't have any snake zombies).

Keeping my bottom palm flat, I slapped my other into it, not unlike a gator chomp. Dust clouded the air like I was clapping two chalkboard erasers together. I waved my arms around, going for a good spread.

The spriggans weren't smart enough to hold back and the shock from the fire blast had worn off, so they came at me again. At the last second, I scattered the remaining chunks and fangs from my hand, gripped my oversized skull belt buckle, and called the cottonmouths.

The bone dust and snake teeth were ignored by the

vicious fiends for the first few seconds. After that, ignorance was impossible.

Shadows creeped and slithered. They entwined with each other and curled apart. And when a spriggan loomed too close, the shadows even struck.

One, two, three fiends went down, struggling against invisible foes. In the meantime, I piled on. I manifested a hammer of darkness and batted little men away from me. When they scratched, I shadow punched them. Bones splintered in sickening crunches. More often than not, the spriggans would get back up.

The wave pushed at me. They were too stupid to check themselves, and they paid for the blind attack dearly. It takes a lot of energy to solidify the darkness into a weapon, but faced with gruesome death, you find the energy. I battered the little men till their black blood gushed. After a second hit, they were slower to get up. After a third, they could no longer make that choice.

And the snakes didn't let up either. They weren't enormously dangerous to most, just spirits really, but they wreaked havoc with the spriggans. As the cloud of bone dust widened, so too did its effective range. And stupid or not, eventually reality comes knocking and morale turns.

The spriggans scattered. The look of fear on their faces said it all. By my count, I should've halved their numbers, and wounded more. Only new ones continued to spill from the Nether passage.

Usually fights clear out a room. Other times they attract an even larger audience.

Chapter 8

I had to move. Nothing inspired confidence more than reinforcements, and the snake dust was about to settle on the ground and snuff out.

I darted for Orpheus, kneeing a spriggan in the face and barreling over him. The faun was a coward now, pushing his underlings into me, hiding behind them just as he'd instructed Grettle to do with him. I hesitated in frustration, knowing the loss of action could be my undoing. In battle, you need to alter your strategy based on enemy actions. You can't always react, but no plan survives first contact. I turned to the rabbit hole and wondered if I should retreat instead. After all, I didn't have a dog in this fight.

Orpheus saw my consideration and barked for his underlings to cover the exit. Ten more spriggans rushed into the chamber. Thirty of them standing now. Ten covering Orpheus. Ten on the exit. And ten going on the offensive.

I'd never seen this many fiends at once before, let alone

fought them, but at least they were split up. I sneered and considered my odds. With spriggans, getting dirty's inevitable.

I cloaked my fist in shadow. As the first minion came at me, my punch launched him into the air and over the heads of his allies. I bowled the next one over too. When the claws threatened, I phased past them and reset my location a few yards away. Suddenly behind a couple, they didn't see my blows coming.

They crowded around me. I manifested a tendril of shadow and caught a spriggan around the neck. It hissed as I dragged it away, choking it out. And that's when I felt the teeth.

One of the smaller ones had managed to clamp onto my leg with gangly arms. Acting on reflex, I slipped into the shadow. Some things can prevent that once they get ahold of me. Not spriggans, though. They're too small. Too ineffectual at magic. But that didn't mean my flesh vanished from between her teeth. I slipped away from the others and rematerialized, but the small spriggan had come along for the ride.

I winced as her teeth ripped deeper into muscle. I ran my hand through my hair, coating my palm in fresh blood, and cupped the little beastie's face. Blood magic sizzled her flesh. She roared and flung herself away from me, still smoking. Honestly, the bubbly skin was an improvement.

But her friends were uncowed. They replaced her in line like I was giving away free autographs. Fine by me. If the little fuckers wanted blood, I would give it to them.

I pulled my knife from my belt. It wasn't menacing and couldn't match the damage of Throok's kukri or even Orpheus' boomerang-hatchet. That wasn't its purpose. The knife was ceremonial. A curved blade of bronze with intricate ornamentation. It was a spell token. An implement of black magic.

I slashed the blade across my upper arm and opened a small gash. I know what you're thinking: why use my blood when I could use theirs? But Netherling blood is black and spoiled. It's a vile substance that doesn't conduct the Intrinsics properly. Makes you wonder where silvans get their juice from.

I pooled the red essence in my hand and flung it at my attackers. It burnt like acid. Only minor damage, maybe, but it turned their screams up a notch and caused their ranks to panic. I scooped up an errant cottonmouth fang from the floor. Newly armed by fresh blood, I threw it at a particularly beefy spriggan. The tooth embedded into his neck, and his already-gray skin went black as the magical venom did its work.

Something hammered my back and forced me to my knees. I spun and barely ducked the second swing of a club wielded by an unusually resourceful spriggan. This guy stood out because his clothes were less moldy than the rest. King of the peasants, over here.

He took his club with two hands and swung it overhead. I didn't want to rely on shadow since I was afraid there was something special with the weapons down here, so I blocked the attack with my armored forearm. The flare of blue bedazzled my opponent. It was the last thing he saw, unless you count my ceremonial knife. It slid right into his eye like a plump tomato and the spriggan immediately collapsed.

Sometimes, magic's overrated.

The unsheathed knife didn't wanna let go of the eyeball and I had nasty flashbacks of kebab night. I wiped the blade clean as the spriggan ranks increased. The rabbit hole had a full twenty guarding it now, and several of the ones I'd downed were fighting through the pain and getting back up.

In retrospect, Orpheus hadn't been kidding about the whole "we" angle. He had his own personal army.

Luckily for Ceela and Throok, it was a spriggan army. Too weak to venture outside the Nether, without the magical chops to conceal themselves, and lacking the fortitude to survive overground. The one thing I knew they wouldn't do—*couldn't* do—was follow her outside.

Which was exactly why they were blocking my exit. They didn't want me to escape either. I should've shifted right through them when I had the chance. Now, the shadow couldn't carry me through that many of them.

I considered the underground passage that Orpheus hadn't come from. To be honest, I liked that option even less. Wandering through the Nether was like following will-o'-the-wisps. More likely than not you'd end up a cautionary example in someone's fairy tale (and I'm talking the original ones with the dark endings).

But there was a third option. Orpheus. He was the key to it all.

I blinked through the shadow to shake the spriggans

engaging me. Orpheus locked his animal eyes on me first. Behind the pack of spriggans, he thought he was safe. But shadows follow everybody.

I snaked a tendril from beneath the faun and wrapped it around his horns. When I pulled, my shadow snapped like a rubber band. Orpheus barely jerked his head.

And that's when I got it. The faun's winding horns had a surface of elaborate patterns. Intricate, almost like spellcraft. Except it was innate. Natural. The horns were the source of his power and immune to my shadow magic. His boomerang must've been carved from the same material. I guess voodoo animists like me haven't cornered the market on using the dead.

My steps toward Orpheus were determined. I rammed a bowling ball of darkness ahead to clear the way. I skipped through the shadow—left, then right—keeping the fiends guessing as to my location. Right before my final jump, I gripped the cut on my arm and squeezed thick blood into my palm. I wiped it on both hands and prepared my spell. The shadows took me, and before anyone knew what had happened, I materialized behind Orpheus and grabbed him by the horns.

The warm blood on my hands was a conduit for my power. It smoked and crackled as it contacted the silvan's horn, but I locked my grip like a vise. I yanked his man-goat head so far back Orpheus almost fell over, but he steadied as he felt the tip of my bronze blade at his throat.

"Call off your army," I said, "or I'll cut your horns off and sell them on the black market."

The faun grimaced and I heard a gasp. Behind me, Grettle had her hand over her mouth. She wanted to say something, but Orpheus held up clawed fingers and the activity in the room ground to a halt. The horde of spriggans fell silent save for scattered moans from the fallen. Grettle took a step backward into shadow.

"Don't do anything stupid," said Orpheus.

"Clear the way!" I commanded. Left hand on the horn, right hand on the knife, I dragged him toward the rabbit hole.

The faun glowered. "My people will never forgive any harm against me."

"Do I look bothered?"

"I don't mean the spriggans, human. I mean my kin, the Circle of Bone. I am a baron in their ranks. A great benefactor."

I rolled my eyes. "You sound real important. Tell your grunts to clear the way if they want to keep being benefacted."

He growled and I yanked his head back further. I wasn't certain he was completely helpless—silvans are renowned for their trickery—but he seemed to play things safe at least. He nodded to the crowd of beasties guarding the exit, and they grumbled and stood aside.

The blood on my hand popped and my palm began to burn. I clenched my jaw and gripped Orpheus tighter before spinning us both around to address the room. "I'm not here for a fight. I don't care about fauns or satyrs or underground holes. If I don't see another spriggan or minotaur for the rest of my life, I'll be a happy man."

The faun twisted his scruffy lips into a smile. "Who said anything about a minotaur?"

I paused, realizing he hadn't mentioned that part to me. By the slowly darkening complexion of his face, it was obvious he hadn't known.

"A minotaur?" he growled, incredulous. Orpheus shook in my grip and my hand smoked. His power was burning off my magic at a fast clip. Soon I wouldn't be able to hold him down. That's what I got for talking.

"Settle down!" I barked, jerking him to the side. A brave spriggan crept too close and I split his nose with an alligator boot. At the far end of the room, Grettle held her breath as she watched us.

My voice softened. "You can come with me," I told her.

"Like hell," said Orpheus, narrowing his eyes. "You think we're subservient to wizards down here? Our people are warriors, as stout as any trickle of power you possess."

"Quiet," I said, staring at the plain-faced woman.

Grettle blinked her lost eyes and a line formed on her forehead. Then she shook her head and backed down the tunnel.

"Grettle," I called.

Orpheus chuckled. "Don't be forlorn, human. You will see us again, if you so wish."

"If I see you again I'll mount your head on my mantle." What? Everglades hideaways could have mantles.

The faun sneered. "Human, I am the great Orpheus. Your insults I can concede to ignorance, but your threats will be met in kind." He twisted his head and spat on the floor. "The Nether knows you now."

The heat on my left hand increased. "That's all right. I don't plan on coming back." I addressed the crowd again. "Now, here's what's going to happen. I'm gonna go topside. Any faun or spriggan or even spider that follows me out will be met with deadly force. Is that clear?"

The horde of fiends shuffled listlessly as if they couldn't comprehend the situation. It's not like they could go out anyway. And Grettle was gone.

Orpheus, for his part, chuckled deeply, almost as if I no longer mattered. My hand gripping the horn was shaking now, knuckles white with effort, and my palm began to sear like a rib eye.

I pulled up right to the exit, put my boot to his backside, and kicked the baron to the ground. He halted his laughter at the affront, but the smile never abandoned his face.

"You are known to us now, human," he repeated. "You bear my mark."

I wiped my aching hand on my jeans and then upturned it to see the magical swirls from his horn branded into my flesh, right on top of my palm tattoo.

Orpheus boomed loud with laughter. "A night, a day. It matters nay. A pox, a curse, sealed with a verse. That is the Nether promise."

Hell, I didn't like the sound of that at all.

Shakespeare over there didn't move, but the horde of spriggans closed in. I vaulted backward into the rabbit hole, through the magical portal between steppes, and once again tumbled on my ass.

It was undignified, but I was back in the Everglades.

I rolled back into the grass and scooped my shotgun from the shadow. With the speed of a trained soldier, or at least an inebriated one, I loaded the first shell I fingered and stabbed the sawed off toward the tree and the not-so-harmless nook between its roots, waiting for something—anything—to emerge.

The short barrel jerked back and forth unsteadily. The right hand wasn't the wounded one, but something much more primal than a contact burn was causing my arm to shake.

Chapter 9

I crept through the wild, soured by the turn of events. Mud in my boots, my best friend hunting me down, and then the silvans. They were in their own class of trouble. Orpheus was a real piece of work—a magical boomerang, spriggan groupies, and even a runaway in a nightgown—but I had to give the crown to Ceela. Her innocent act had fooled me good.

"Just deny seeing us," I mocked in her voice. Cisco Suarez, the sucker for a nose wiggle. The satyr had set me up to battle Orpheus and cover her escape. My detour in the Nether left me spent, bloodied, and with a silvan curse for my trouble. Not really a list of things you look for in a hiding place.

But Ceela and Throok had come through. My original problem was the police, and I didn't see any sign of them in or around my boathouse. The cavalry had been called off and my possessions were safe. The best part was, if the silvans were true to their word, I wouldn't need to worry about any more midnight visits.

That didn't mean the cops would let up. No doubt, they wanted me bad. Even with Evan commanding them, the DROP team was in hard pursuit. And from the conversation I overheard, his command was somewhat precarious. Evan was in hot water with the commissioner. That sergeant was gunning for his job. The cause of that friction? Yours truly.

You see, Evan's unit is a special appointment. Politically driven, which means susceptible to corruption. I didn't think my friend was especially dirty, but the directives handed down to him were chock full of ulterior motives. For all his self-righteousness, Lieutenant Evan Cross had the right blend of naivety and loyalty to turn a blind eye. What I hoped he was finally understanding was that certain people wanted me dead, off the books.

They say if you wanna make enemies, try to change something. Unfortunately, there isn't any infinite wisdom for what to do once you piss off a bent city commissioner.

I left the Everglades as the morning broke. My pickup truck was in the shop again, so I hitched a ride on *Calle Ocho* and headed into Miami proper.

I would've called my friend Milena, but she wasn't talking to me. She's beautiful and strong and amazing, but she'd had too much. Ironic. We were chased across Miami Beach by a homicidal poltergeist and she didn't bat an eye, but she came face to face with my dark past and rightfully backed away. I didn't blame her. Cisco Suarez was in the disappointment business. Besides, she was safer without me.

My ride dropped me off at the mechanic. I paid cash for

my truck and drove off. The behemoth of a pickup was born in the 1970s, back when they made things out of metal. Its tan paint would've been faded if it hadn't been overtaken by a sheen of rust. The radio was ripped out. The engine knocking was gone. It was about as far from "like new" as possible but it could take a beating. Besides, I kind of liked its quirks.

After a left turn, my blinker didn't shut off, even when I flipped it manually. All right, "quirks" was a bad word. Maybe I failed to mention that my pickup is kinda, technically, haunted.

I'd been hounded by more than a few ghosts lately, comeuppance for the same dark past that scared Milena off. Here's your Final Jeopardy answer: This leaves a trail of pissed-off and magically-inclined dead bodies in its wake.

What is a zombie hit man, Alex?

Needless to say, I'd been kept on my toes, banishing whatever spirits came at me. Most of them were long gone now, but the ghost who'd latched onto my truck was a stubborn one. A weak shadow of his old self. In time, the frequent tune-ups would no longer be necessary.

I made my way along Biscayne Bay and parked outside City Hall. There I sat. And sat. And waited. And sat. All for a man named Rudi Alvarez. He must've gotten an early start because I didn't see him roll in. When lunchtime came around and the city commissioner didn't emerge, I realized he was playing hooky. Where would he be if not at work?

I started the truck on the first try, headed to Pinecrest, and circled the block of Rudi's manorial home. The place looked nice. Groundskeeping staff was busy restoring the property. New flowers planted, the pond cleared and refilled. The metal skeleton of a new greenhouse frame was already being rebuilt.

It was fast work, and a far cry from the barren battlefield of two weeks ago. The one that had drawn me into the public eye and earned me a most-wanted poster. But now, evidence of that little scuffle was nearly erased. Interesting how easily life rolls on with money.

Even more interesting was the state of security—or rather, the lack of it. After the incidents at his house and City Hall, the politician's security was beefed up. He'd surrounded himself with bodyguards. Not animists, though (from what I could tell). Rudi didn't have the juice for that, which is what made his situation so curious.

Believe it or not, I don't play Miami politics. I don't watch the news. I don't vote. I leave all that to the huddled masses. So why my interest in a city commissioner, one of five who control their own tactical police unit?

Rudi was just a pawn, really. No spellcraft, no smarts. Just a handsome face and a firm handshake. He was a puppet for my true enemy: the Covey.

One day, ten years ago, I boarded a boat to meet the Covey. They dragged me off it half dead, and later finished the job. The Covey was a ragtag band of misfit animists and Nether creatures who conspired to grow powerful. Best I could make out was they wanted the Horn of Subjugation to make inroads into the Miami voodoo community. They used me to find it, and then gutted me and turned me into their undead servant. But not before I hid the artifact from them.

It was a small win, but life as a zombie hit man did a number on every relationship I ever had. But what would life be, or death for that matter, if it couldn't surprise you?

As a budding black magic animist myself, I surprised everybody with a secret spell on my dying breath. It was Cisco spellcraft, with a capital C. Not the curse of a Spanish wraith. Not the voodoo or obeah or vampiric compulsions. Those all worked me over good all right, but the kiss of black magic that hung over my life for the next ten years was my own.

Spellcraft not to rise from the dead so much as to fake it. Or welcome it temporarily. I killed myself to keep others from doing so, to protect myself and the Horn from prying supernatural eyes. Sure, I was their zombie bitch anyway, but it was a charade put into motion by *my* magic.

Now that spellcraft is done. Dried up like an old well. The various hexes I was under were predicated on my being dead—when that was no longer true, I was me again. Cisco Suarez. Alive, and stronger for it, but with a hot mess of baggage. A best friend who'd married my girlfriend to help raise and protect the daughter I never knew. The girlfriend who was part of the Covey, who'd manipulated me from the beginning to find the Taíno artifact. Worst of all was the smothering guilt I felt for murdering my own family at the behest of an unrelenting and uncompromising undead compulsion.

That was what the Covey did to me. *That* is who they are.

And *that's* why I'm going to destroy every single one of them.

The obeah man was the first to die. I killed him while he spun his dark ritual, before I ever cursed myself to death.

The anansi trickster spider fell after I returned to life, burned down in the house of my murdered childhood associate.

Next came Tunji Malu, the asanbosam, a West African vampire. It was his vampiric compulsion that I served for ten years. His will that I followed. I snapped his neck and incinerated him to ash, his metal teeth the only evidence he ever existed.

Those were the simple ones.

The rest of the Covey was a harder nut to crack. Cunning and strength have played roles, no doubt, but my true obstacle was following the web of deceit they'd built in their time in Miami. The shadow play. Nigerian business fronts. A gang war incited in Little Haiti. These things led me to the politician who benefited from the conspiracy of belly-up real estate.

And that was why I was back in Miami proper, risking discovery from the "enhanced" police patrols. Rudi Alvarez wasn't an animist or a Nether creature, but he had plenty of power. It was his order that sent the DROP team to my door. He was the one with the political muscle to become mayor and own this city. Instead of taking my offer of truce, he was coming at me with everything he had. In my book, that makes him one of them, puppet or not.

Puppet strings are hard to see but, if you know what to

look for, they can lead you right to the puppeteer.

But first I needed to locate the puppet. Rudi's security wasn't at his house, which meant he wasn't either. The commissioner was on lockdown, his staff disappeared and out of reach. That made for days of surveillance without yield. My investigation had pretty much ground to a halt.

Frustrating considering how close Rudi had gotten to me last night. If the Covey was going to turtle up, I had to change my strategy.

I opened the glove compartment and pulled out a spare burner phone. I use several to stay ahead of modern surveillance, but sometimes stealth is overrated. I dialed the direct line to the commander of the team tasked with hunting me down.

Chapter 10

"Cross," said my buddy as he answered the phone.

Evan wasn't my first choice for an ally these days. As a general rule, best friends don't lead midnight raids against each other.

"What's your boss playing at?" I asked calmly.

"C-Cisco?" he stuttered, correcting his voice to a whisper. I heard him put the receiver on the desk and shut his office door. When he picked up again, he said, "You have a lot of nerve calling here. You know that?"

"You mad because your nighttime romp in the Everglades wasn't fruitful?"

"I... The... We were just spinning our wheels."

My friend's tone betrayed confusion, like he wasn't sure where I meant. Maybe the silvans hadn't been pulling my leg after all.

I got straight to the point. "You wanna tell me what you're doing running a hit squad?"

"What?"

"I'm threatening to expose the commissioner's corrupt dealings—the manufactured gang war, the property values—all of it. They need me dead or they'll be exposed. You see that, right? They're using your team to justify my murder."

The lieutenant's voice was sharp. "We're police officers, goddamn it. Not assassins. We're going to find you, Cisco. I promise you that much. But you'll be in handcuffs, not a body bag."

I scoffed. "You sure about that?"

"Of course I am."

"You'd put my life in the hands of Sergeant Garcia? The guy who wants your job? Who wants to impress the brass at any cost?"

My friend finally had no comeback. I hoped the silence was him being sympathetic to my cause.

"What do they know about me?" I asked.

"What?"

"They know my name," I explained. "Cisco."

"Yeah. They heard me call you that at the standoff two weeks ago. It would've been suspicious except Commissioner Alvarez knew your name too. Apparently you walked right up to him and introduced yourself."

I shrugged. "I'm a personable guy. So what else do they know?"

I could practically hear Evan shaking his head in disbelief. "Why should I tell you?"

"Because people will get hurt, buddy. My family, Martine, everybody the Covey knew I was in contact with is dead. Or in your case, threatened and underhand."

Evan cleared his throat. "Covey? What are you talking about?"

"Keep up, Evan. The people behind this. My death. The threats against your family to keep you in line. You didn't think these were the actions of one rogue vampire, did you?"

"You're talking about your political conspiracy theory again."

I hissed in frustration. "I'm telling you, these people have their hooks in your boss. Commissioner Alvarez is as dirty as they are. His head of security is a freaking volcanic elemental."

"Tyson Roderick was fired after the fiasco at the house."

Fired? I didn't know elementals could be fired. I did know they were damned hard to kill. Tyson was taken out twice, but it hadn't stuck.

"They're just covering their tracks, Evan. What about his chief of staff?"

"You mean Kita."

"Yes. Kita Mariko. She was part of that backyard brawl too. She's an animist, man."

"She's Emily's half sister," he spat.

I paused. There was the rub. I reached in my back pocket and pulled out the bent photograph of Emily. "You know about that?"

"I... I found out. I didn't lie to you, Cisco."

I figured as much. When I'd first set my sights on Kita, Evan told me she and Emily were merely friends. But this was Emily we're talking about. My lying ex-girlfriend. She was part of the Covey that had me killed. Meanwhile, Evan barely believed in the group's existence. It wasn't a stretch to think that Emily had lied to her husband about a number of things.

This was ground I had to tread carefully.

"You don't find it suspicious that Emily's keeping secrets?"

"It was Kita's secret," he stressed.

"A pretty vital secret considering—"

"I'm not having this conversation, Cisco." Evan's tone took a hard edge. He was fiercely protective of his family. To be honest, I admired the trait. (He was raising my daughter after all.) But perhaps it made him blind to their faults. His wife, her sister, they weren't who he thought they were.

Problem was, Evan would never believe my word over hers. I couldn't tell him what his wife was guilty of or risk turning him against me for good.

I folded down the pickup's sun visor. A photocopy was paper clipped to it: the registration of the boat I'd been practically killed on. Intelligence garnered from my friendship with Evan. To me, his help proved he was on my side, at least somewhat. I couldn't lose that support completely.

I slid the picture of Emily under the paper clip. I still didn't know how to confront her betrayal, even as the subject of a conversation.

Eyes on the prize, Cisco. I needed to forget about my ex. I changed the subject.

"Where's Rudi?"

"This is a joke, right?"

"It's no joke," I said. "The commissioner hasn't been at home or work for a few days."

"I know that, Cisco. Alvarez is out of the country. The joke is that you think I'm your source in the police department or something."

"Where did he go?"

"You're not listening to me, man. I'm not telling you where my boss is. That's only gonna lead to trouble."

"What about Kita? Can I talk to her?"

Evan laughed defiantly into the receiver. "You kidding? You better not get anywhere near her, man. Besides, she's out of town too. I'll tell her to send you a postcard from the beach."

I gritted my teeth. My confidence in Evan's support was waning. "Give me something, man."

My friend took a long breath. "I don't know anything about this Covey. I'm a police officer. I do my job. If you want to know what the police know of your identity, it's a first name. That's it. You don't have a social security number or a credit card or an address. All semblance of an identity is lost on you. I'm the only one that knows your background, and as far as I'm concerned, it all stays in the past. We're chasing a ghost."

I smiled at the thought, but I couldn't enjoy it. For all I knew, Evan was keeping my past a secret because he was inextricably tied to it. His men would never forgive him if he was outed as the best friend of their top target, even if the title was a decade-old standby.

"Good," I told him. "I'm not coming after your guys. I don't want the police coming after me."

"What are you saying? You're done?"

"Far from it, bro. Rudi Alvarez, the Covey—they're fair game. Anyone that had a hand in the death of my family is going down."

Evan nearly had an aneurysm over the phone. "You can't walk around Miami like some crazed vigilante, Cisco. There needs to be order. Justice."

"My family's been dead for eight years. I've had it with lawful justice. I'm on my own now."

"We'll stop you."

I clenched my jaw. "You'll try."

Evan Cross sighed in frustration. "You don't get it. The resources of the City of Miami Police Department will be brought to bear. You messed with the big dogs, Cisco. The politicians may not know anything about magic, but they have their own kind of power. You can't stand up to that alone."

"Then work with me."

"I told you, I'm a police officer. If you're concerned this is gonna end in a shoot-out, turn yourself in. You'll be safe."

"I'll be in a cell."

"But alive. And we can sort out the injustices then."

Sort out. Jeez. They say justice is blind, but Evan was deluding himself. "My story can never come out. I was declared dead. Even if we somehow made it past that, I'd have countless murders laid at my feet for being a hit man. I don't think the mindless-zombie defense will hold up in court."

"Then bring us proof," he pleaded. "Not of the magic. Like you said, that will never happen. But give me something against this Covey that will hold up in court."

I flexed my burnt palm open and closed. The burn marks had darkened, and they hurt like a bitch. "If you're serious about that you'd give me a place to start looking. Kita's his chief of staff. Let's start with where she is."

He scoffed. "Jesus. You don't give up with this. You can't go after her. She's family and she works for my boss. Hurting her is like hurting me, brother."

"Says the guy leading my manhunt. I'm just looking for evidence. Like you said."

"I'm not gonna let you hurt her, Cisco."

I sighed. "I promise to play nice. This is about getting evidence. Proving there's a conspiracy."

"That's right. I won't give you Kita, but give me a paper trail, and I'll give you justice."

I considered my friend's words. "Maybe you will," I told him. I hung up the phone.

Fat lot of good my police contact was. It's no wonder I'm an outlaw.

I stared at the commissioner's house, wondering what country he could run to. I mean, he was a politician. He couldn't just disappear without a trace, right?

Since my conversation with Evan had gone so well, I figured I'd go two-for-two with the direct approach. (I know. I'm a sucker for punishment.) It took a couple phone calls to get the right line to City Hall, but I found it. In the meantime, one of the groundskeepers on Rudi's property threw nervous glances my way. I was pulled over on the side of the road just outside his fence. Despite the tree cover, he'd made me. I guess an old pickup like mine stands out in a town like this.

"The office of Commissioner Alvarez," came a woman's throaty voice over the phone. It wasn't the good kind of throaty that seduced men—more the pack-a-day kind. "What is this regarding?"

"Um, hello. My firm is interested in making a campaign donation."

"You must mean the Passport to Latin America," she said matter-of-factly. "What company do you represent?"

"Well, I'd like to keep that confidential until the time is right."

"Of course, sir. Are you representing national or international interests?"

I smiled. "South Florida, through and through."

"Happy to hear it, sir." It sounded like she was writing something down.

The groundskeeper who spotted me took another hard look my way. He headed to the house and knocked on the door. I tensed.

"Ma'am, I was hoping to speak to Commissioner Alvarez as soon as possible."

"I'm afraid that won't be possible before the fund-raiser. The commissioner is visiting with partners in the Cayman Islands, but I can schedule you for next week. I do need to know your name and affiliation, of course."

I made crackly noises with my mouth and ended the call. In retrospect, it was probably more obvious than just hanging up.

Son of a bitch. The Cayman Islands. Rudi's bank account that harbored the funds from his illicit real estate scheme was in the Caymans. But that wasn't all. I pulled out the slip of paper under Emily's picture. The boat that had been found with my blood all over it. It was registered in the Caymans. How had I missed that link before?

The front door opened and the groundskeeper pointed me out to a man in a suit. A skeleton security staff had been left behind. So much for the stake out.

As the man in the suit made his way across the yard, I tossed the burner out the truck window and sped away before he could get a clear look. But it wasn't him I was worried about.

I knew Evan about as well as you could know a person. We'd been through a lot growing up. He was still my friend, but he was also a family man and cop. No doubt he was working on tracking my phone the second I'd hung up.

Let them. The police would wind up at Rudi's house, and the warning would be clear: come to my house and I'll come to yours.

Chapter 11

My pickup is registered in the name of the old man who sold it to me. It was a cash transaction without transfer of ownership. That makes it untraceable to me. As long as no one links me to the vehicle, I can drive around without fear of a BOLO. I doubted the security guard at the commissioner's house knew who I was or caught the make of the truck, much less the plate. That was good enough for me as I made my way down South Dixie Highway, planning a Caribbean vacation.

US 1 is the longest north-south highway in the country, running all the way from the Canadian border in Maine to the southernmost tip of the United States in Key West. The Florida Keys are practically Caribbean islands themselves. Some large, some small; some built from trash; all connected by the land bridge that is US 1. The northernmost and largest of the islands is Key Largo. Less than an hour out of Miami, that's where I was, pulling into the driveway of a charter company.

The building had seen better days. Broken windows shoddily repaired with plywood, a warped wooden sign with an unreadable company logo, a mailbox rusted by the salty coastal air—I was beginning to think I should've called before making the trip down.

I hopped out of the truck and made my way to the porch. Old floorboards creaked beneath me, but I wasn't sure there was anyone home to note my presence. I was proven wrong by the sound of a shotgun pumping its action.

"Cisco Suarez," came a shrill voice from behind the screen door.

I put my hands up slowly and peered inside. I couldn't see anyone in the darkness. I let the black leak into my eyes again, and the interior began to illuminate.

"Don't you be trying that shadow squat with me, brujo."

I pulled my head back, surprised the woman had noticed. Even with my enhanced sight, I could barely make her out through the dusty screen door. "Just trying to get a good look at you, is all."

"Hmph. Why didn't you say that? Take a step back."

I did.

The door swung open and Carla emerged. I was right about the shotgun. Ten or twelve gauge, double barrel, pointed at my chest.

I sighed loudly. "You know that's next to useless against me, right?"

"I like the weight of it all the same," she replied.

Despite being in her mid fifties, Carla was a woman of action. Underneath her sun-leathered skin were tight, ropey muscles. She had tan hair that barely reached her eyes or covered her ears, and a hard face that meant business.

"What in Jesus' asshole do you want?" she snapped.

Oh, and she had a mouth only a deaf mother could love.

But what in Jesus' asshole *did* I want? Well, Carla was a smuggler, or had been when I'd known her years ago. She had a boat and she was an illusionist, which were a couple things I really needed right now.

Sure, I could turtle up in my hideout and hope the silvan magic would keep me out of sight, but I wouldn't make forward progress sitting on my ass. Two weeks of failed stake outs attested to that. Better to look for a needle in a Caribbean island.

"You still taking on clients?" I asked.

Her eyes hardened. "I went to jail 'cause of you."

"You went to jail because you tried to smuggle out a poser Jamaican witch doctor who robbed charms from my partner."

Her head shot back, as if she'd never thought of the situation with as much clarity before. "You blew up my boat and crashed it into a Navy vessel!"

"Whoa, whoa. *You* crashed your boat after *my powder* blew it up. I wasn't the one who took it onboard. Besides, the fire burned away the drug stash I know your client was carrying. You could say I saved you from trafficking charges."

"Hmph. That's a fist up my ass if I ever had one."

Breathtaking imagery. "Carla, what are we talking about here anyway? You paid a fine and were put on probation. It could've been much worse. From the looks of it, you're still in business."

"The business of taking a dump," she answered, and I hoped that was colorful language. "I look like I'm making a respectable income here?"

I smiled and pulled a fold of cash from my jeans.

Carla dropped the shotgun to her side. "Shit. Why the hell you wait so long to take those bills out?"

As the old smuggler counted the money, I told her what I needed. She shrugged like it was nothing and counted the cash again. I kept quiet until she finished this time. Better not to make someone holding a shotgun lose count.

Within the hour, Carla walked me to the dock to help load the boat. It was a forty-two-foot yacht. Not a whole lot of upper cabin space but it looked fast. Maybe not luxury, per se, but it was worth a king's ransom compared to the building she lived in.

I was a little uneasy stepping aboard. The last time I walked on a boat, I didn't walk off in one piece. Good thing I had no memory of that incident or I might be afraid of sailing.

"Seas are calm today," Carla said. "Four-foot waves at most. That keeps up, I'll get us there in a day and a half."

I raised my eyebrows. "A day and a half? This thing has an engine, right?"

"Don't be an oaf," she snapped. "This is the fastest I've got. Had to sell my go-fast. Damn shame, too, but radar technology's caught up with 'em anyway."

I chuckled. If there was a living pirate in Key Largo, it

was her.

Not only that, but her yacht, the *Now You See Me*, was a veritable ghost ship. It was trim and clean and didn't have spirits of creepy British children, but Carla's magic ensured it had a few tricks. Namely, her illusory spellcraft could make it practically disappear, given the right conditions.

We loaded up and hit the high seas. I wasn't much of a sailor, but after years of death and weeks of being a fugitive, being on the open ocean was a relief. Birds hovered on the breeze overhead. Dolphins swam in the aqua below. I watched the sun set over the open water and deepen the landscape to a brilliant cerulean, beautiful yet mysterious.

But even though the water was relatively calm, it was choppier than the ride in my pickup. My insides tightened and I began focusing less on the beauty of the earth and more on keeping my lunch down. And that's a slow way to pass the time.

We stopped to refuel in Havana, then again in Cape Antonio, before making a beeline to Grand Cayman. The stops were a welcome break from the monotony of the sea, but I never disembarked. I hid in the shadows and got what sleep I could.

By the next morning, my excitement had built again. I made a point to watch the sunrise, and the water was a deeper green than anything I'd seen in my life. We were almost at our destination and I was already getting nostalgic about the journey. A little sea sickness is a welcome price to pay for shoving the stresses of reality aside.

Carla sat on her captain's chair picking at the calluses on

her bare feet. Despite that, I tried to capture the serenity by staring into the sea. But it was gone already. My elusive white whale, sunken in the depths of my burgeoning investigation.

The Covey. The remaining living members were in a holding pattern. Hiding from me. Except for Emily. She was in plain sight but, in many ways, the most difficult to deal with.

Em. The love of my other life. After going off and dying, I couldn't really blame her for marrying my best friend, but to find out she was part of the Covey? To discover the only reason she ever introduced herself was to manipulate a naive shadow witch into finding the Horn of Subjugation and then steal it for herself? That hit me hard.

Like a sap, I reached for the picture in my back pocket. I was happy to find I'd left it in the pickup. But that didn't stop my thoughts.

In some ways, Emily was a complete stranger now. For all I knew, she was an animist herself. But there were still some acts I couldn't reconcile, some facts that made me believe Emily wasn't all bad. She'd apologized about my parents, claiming not to have a hand in that. She'd named our daughter after me and given her the doll I gifted. These were strange actions for a heartless conspirator.

Maybe I was just another sucker who wanted to believe, allowing remnants of my love for her to cloud my judgment. But it was what it was. Emily still had a hold on me, still tugged my heartstrings. She sat at home everyday, out in the open, but how could I harm the mother of my child?

Women, am I right?

Her half sister was a different matter. Kita Mariko, the offspring of an Australian real estate tycoon and a Japanese mistress. Em never told me about her half sister, but I connected the dots. Really, the dots were connected for me. Shoved into my face by the poltergeist of their dead father. The cover story presented his death as an accident, but Kita and Emily had conspired in his death to take over his land holdings in the Caribbean. How Kita had forced her sister into that situation was beyond me.

The man was another victim of my undead hand. Another drop of guilt in my bucket. Thinking over the connection of their well-traveled father convinced me that coming out here was all the more necessary. But I had to be careful.

Kita Mariko is Commissioner Alvarez's chief of staff, but she's much more than a bureaucrat. She's an animist. A paper mage. Interesting magic and the reason I now always carry flammable shells on hand. After our confrontation at the commissioner's house, I suspected Kita was the brains of the operation. Maybe she'd brainwashed Emily somehow.

There I went again. Looking for excuses.

But the Horn, killing me, killing their father—they were all just plays at something larger. Something that entailed buying a politician and the soon-to-be mayor of Miami. As the man's chief of staff, Kita was invaluable. Without her around, the Covey's influence was neutralized.

That only left Tyson Roderick, the ousted head of security for the commissioner. The real mystery behind the man was why a volcanic elemental was engaged in Earthly politics.

Elementals are strange creatures. I'd butted heads with Tyson. Killed him even. But that just banished him to his plane temporarily. Nothing stopped him from coming back again. Only so far, he hadn't come back. And if he didn't come to me I could hardly go to him. Not where he lives.

Opposed to the Nether, elementals are from the Aether. It's a steppe above ours. A place of primal beings. Jinns, dragons, and elementals. The Aether is made of fire and air, and it's a place humans cannot tread.

I sulked as I watched the water and the deep. The Nether is the polar opposite of the Aether. The Nether is made of earth and water, a land of silvans, giants, and fiends. Much more familiar to our kind. Much more tangible and material.

I considered my empty palm, scarred with blackened lines making up arcane shapes. The wound had scabbed over with a black crust. I hoped that meant my enhanced healing was going to work on it, but I wasn't optimistic. This was no ordinary burn.

Not ten feet from me, a serpent-like creature wriggled under the turquoise waves. Its timing, as I pondered the Nether, was impeccably creepy. Just as mythical creatures can venture through rabbit holes on land, Nether beings live beneath the sea as well. They're all around us. Under us. But they know how to stay out of sight. After my silvan curse, I knew to stay out of the Nether as well.

Carla stomped over to me. "If you're gonna puke, just do

it already. I don't want you embarrassing me in sight of land."

I snapped out of my thoughts and noticed the island in view, flat and difficult to see, but taking up more and more of the horizon as we closed in. I quickly ducked below the rail. Time to get down to business.

"I'm fine," I told her. "What's the plan?"

Carla's weathered eyes considered me. "What plan?"

"I mean, how are you gonna get me in? I figure you can make me invisible while I follow you through customs."

"Angel farts," she snapped. "If I could work illusions on people, you think I'd keep this mug?"

I arched an eyebrow. "So, what then? Some kind of Trojan horse play? Or maybe a distraction. I could blow something up."

"Hell, no. What is it with you and explosions? What we're doing is much easier than that." The Key Largo pirate reached into her boat shorts and handed me a passport. "Here you go."

I checked the ID. It was a near-perfect recreation of what I assumed to be a modern passport, complete with a picture of me that I had never posed for. I could sense the ambient Intrinsics emanating from the paper, and wondered what was really printed on it.

"I've never had a passport before," I whispered.

And just like that, Cisco Suarez was official.

Chapter 12

Grand Cayman's not a huge island, but upon leaving the clutches of the expansive sea and sky, it felt like it was all the land in the world. The white sand clashed against the rainbow of blues above and below, but it was far from an idyllic scene of pure, natural beauty. Tourists with sunburns scurried around madly like panicked ants. Locals hawked wares with impolite sales tactics. These were the vacation highlights edited out of movie reels.

Still, the spirit of the original island remained. A scoundrel's sense of adventure, maybe. Or a potential bounty. I couldn't put my finger on it.

Carla's enchanted passport held up. We made it through customs without a second look, and I wondered if the enchantment had a slight charm to it as well. I didn't have a chance to ask the boat captain because she told me to be back at the dock the next afternoon (but not too early 'cause she likes her beauty sleep) and disappeared without another word.

Guess she wanted no part of my trouble. Guess I didn't blame her.

I was now alone in George Town, the capital of the territory. Despite being nowhere near as sprawling as Miami, I was suddenly daunted and wished I had Carla as a tour guide. I could literally start anywhere.

The Cayman Islands, a sunny place for shady people. When a group of three tiny islands in the middle of the Caribbean makes it into the top five banking centers in the world, you know something's fishy. That's not the same thing as illegal, mind you, but it gets pretty close. Huge corporations to private asset holders all enjoy the light and indirect taxation the Caymans provide, but it really comes down to hiding money.

Why is any of this important to me? Well, the paper trail, Sherlock.

Fact the first: As part of my zombie service, I had helped incite a gang war in the voodoo communities of Little Haiti. The public crime wave spiked media attention. Predictably, property values plummeted. My recent break-in to City Hall had caused all sorts of grief (including an up-close-and-personal police raid), but the visit uncovered proof that Rudi Alvarez and his staff, including Evan, had holdings in a Cayman Islands financial services company named Blue Sky.

Fact the second: Along with my gang warfare, I'd assassinated Australian real-estate tycoon Henry Hoover. His wealth went to his daughter Emily Cross. Most of his estate by then had been long squandered, but various properties in the Caribbean, notably the Cayman Islands, were part of the inheritance.

Finally, and perhaps most important, fact the third: Ten years ago I'd boarded a boat for a date with destiny that led to my capture and death. The boat was registered to a defunct charter company on Grand Cayman (think Carla's small-time operation except on this side of Cuba). The business was long gone, but any possible links were worth checking out while I was in the neighborhood.

I scratched my head and considered my options. Bank accounts, real estate, or the boat I'd been murdered on. Try boring, boring, and about damn time I got answers.

Destination in mind, I hit a local rental shop. The Caymans are a British territory so everybody speaks English. Even better, they accept US cash. That made it easy for me to flash my passport and rent a scooter. One pair of plastic sunglasses later and Cisco Suarez was out for a coastal ride, albeit on the left side of the road.

Within twenty minutes, I got my bearings and made it to the address of Stingray Tours, where the boat had been registered. Except the waterside building wasn't a charter company anymore. It was a scuba shop.

I parked my scooter and entered the storefront. Diving gear lined the shelves and a single old man sat behind the counter.

"Hi there," I said, just another unassuming tourist. "You guys rent boats?"

The geezer arched an eyebrow. "We don't do tours."

It was that obvious I didn't belong. I took the news like a champ. Frowning for a second and then pulling back before

I overplayed the act, I said, "My father told me Stingray Tours was the place to get a charter."

The man widened his eyes. "He must've told you that a while ago, son. Stingray used to do business here but that was years ago. I bought the shop when they went out of business."

"Out of business?" Crestfallen. "Any idea what happened?"

"The owner killed himself on a binger." The man said it like he was talking about a piece of food stuck in his teeth. "His wife was his partner and she died in the crash too. No more backers, no more business."

I shook my head mournfully. "That's too bad. My dad said he had a great time with him."

"Charles? I doubt it. He was a grumpy bastard." Pot, meet kettle. "Your old man must've been talking about Captain Wallace. He was the talkative one. Did most of the tours."

I snapped my fingers. "Wallace. That's it. He still around?"

"Sure is," said the man, losing some edge to his voice. "He's doing his own thing under his own name now. Flipped to the opposite side of the island, but that's not a long drive in these parts."

I pumped the owner for the details, thanked him, and left the shop. I wasn't looking for the boat anymore. Since it had been stolen and impounded by Miami police, it wasn't worth nosing around for physical evidence here. I hopped on the scooter and blazed a trail to Rum Point Beach.

It was a winding route that took me around much of the island, but the old man was right. I made it in less than an hour. I had to ask around to find Wallace Sightseeing. I was glad I did because I wouldn't have found it on my own.

Carla's dilapidated business place was a modern miracle of design compared to Wallace's, which I'd describe as more of a hut or shanty. It didn't have its own dock and no one answered the door. Some stragglers in the mostly residential neighborhood—locals, not tourists—were watching me. So much for breaking in. I smiled and knocked again.

"He's not there," came a voice from the street. It was an older woman pushing a baby stroller. I didn't see a baby.

"You a friend of Captain Wallace?" I asked.

"Not really."

I frowned, wondering where her baby was. "If you're not his friend, how do you know—"

She pointed at the door behind me. "Read the sign."

That's right, I missed the sign posted on the door window, flipped around to read, "On the water," followed by a phone number. World's greatest detective, I am. At least the sightseeing business was still humming. I turned around to thank the woman but she was already halfway down the block. Maybe it was better to avoid women with empty baby strollers. I saved the number on my phone even though I wasn't planning on using it. The kind of questions I had were best done in person and without announcement.

So much for starting with the exciting clues. Captain Wallace could be on the water for most of the day, and I had too much steam under my sails to wait around for him now. I compromised by picking up lunch at a beachside bar called The Wreck. A few conch fritters and a jerk burger later and I gave up on the captain and scooted back to George Town.

It wasn't check-in time yet and I couldn't look into Hoover's properties without a hotel computer, so that left the Blue Sky paper trail. I headed to the financial center downtown and was surprised by the slew of colorful buildings. Even mega-banks were susceptible to the eccentricities of islander life, I supposed.

It wasn't all glitz and glamour, though. After the financial crackdown of the nineties, the Caymans fell on hard times. Gone were the days of lugging around briefcases of cash to disappear. This wasn't the same Grand Cayman because of it. Gangs were on the rise. Crime and murder more commonplace. It was the type of environment that bred desperation.

That said, a financial center's a financial center. It would be naive to believe everything was on the straight and narrow. Especially the building I approached with large, inviting windows and friendly-looking professionals at their desks. Blue Sky Investments.

That's when I realized my conundrum.

Here I was, with no real paper in my possession, dressed in a plain white tank top, jeans, and red cowboy boots, needing access to sensitive financial data that wasn't mine. I supposed it was worth the old college effort, and maybe my style of dress could be attributed to the same islander eccentricities I was surrounded by.

I entered the silent office. It wasn't a traditional bank, really. Large enough for several desks and kiosks, with a back office for heavy hitters. If I had to guess, there were various managers that interacted personally with clients. To me, that meant big money and specially tailored business.

A pretty young woman caught my eye and waved me to sit down. "What can I do for you?" she asked in a British accent.

No time like the present.

"Hi," I started, trying (and failing) to sound as haughty as she did. "I represent a firm interested in moving assets to Blue Sky."

She nodded with a plastic smile. "Which firm is that?"

I cleared my throat. "Actually, I'd prefer to look into your services before I reveal that."

"I'm sure you would," she replied without missing a beat. "But I wouldn't know what kind of package to set you up with unless you divulge your firm's assets."

I nodded. A perfectly acceptable setback. "Let's start north of a million," I said casually.

The woman didn't even blink. "Are the funds currently with another bank?"

I licked my lips to buy time. "Several banks."

"Let's start with those account numbers and we can verify your approval."

I grimaced as politely as I could manage. "Again, I'd prefer not to divulge that yet."

The woman's smile wavered, but she did an admirable job maintaining it. "Mister...?"

"Livingston," I blurted out.

She nodded. "Yes, Mr. Livingston. I'm sorry to disappoint you, but we are unable to work with clients without a pre-approval phase. I suggest you check with your"—sarcastic tone now—"*firm*, and re-engage us if you decide the opportunity is right."

I smiled politely, but the woman came back with an even stronger one. She had me beat at everything. Pleasantries, subtext, even insincerity. I stuttered for a moment until I saw something that took my voice away completely.

Entering the Blue Sky office from the street was a prim Japanese woman, an all-business bureaucrat in a pants suit by the name of Kita Mariko: chief of staff to one Commissioner Rudi Alvarez.

Chapter 13

There was a big problem with Kita Mariko that I may have glossed over. Namely, she was a formidable paper mage. Worse, she'd recognize me.

Flustered, I swiped at a random tchotchke on the bank manager's desk. A sky-colored stress ball with the company logo on it bounced to the floor. I shot my head below the desk to grab it.

"Is Douglas in the back?" asked Kita as she strolled by the desk.

"Yes," answered the British voice in a decidedly less superior tone. I guess money *does* buy respect.

Kita's heels didn't slow their tempo as she disappeared into the back room. I lifted my head above the desk and let out a sigh of relief.

"Cute," I said, squishing the stress ball a few times. It didn't help. "What's the minimum deposit I need to get one of these? A hundred K?"

The manager crossed her arms and arched her eyebrow,

clearly unamused. I set the stress ball on her desk so the words "Blue Sky" were upside down, excused myself, and hurried outside.

Kita Mariko: disappeared, lying low, doing some good old-fashioned Cayman Islands banking. So much for boring.

I waited on my scooter a block away for twenty minutes until Rudi Alvarez's chief of staff left the building. My eyes followed her to a modest rental car. She sat in the driver's seat of the compact and drove off, never noticing me in tow.

Ten minutes later we were cruising along West Bay Road, along a strip of swanky hotels. Not boutiques, mind you, but giant resorts each one. This was the main destination strip of the island. Loads of money and luxury lined a public beach that had no business looking so beautiful. For a moment, I understood how all the New York snowbirds in South Beach felt, stunned by a strong cocktail of weather and view. But the pleasantries didn't last long. My mark turned into the entrance of a grand hotel with a name I couldn't pronounce.

Kita exited the car with a black satchel strapped across her back. She tossed her keys to the valet and marched through the high glass doors without glancing back. She was confident, with the air of someone who'd been here awhile and done this before.

What had Rudi Alvarez's office said? Something about accepting campaign donations for Latin America. He wasn't just hiding. This was business as usual for him and his staff. And I'd thought he fled Miami because of little old me. Talk about a hit to my ego.

After my experience with the bank manager, I couldn't handle a judgmental look from the valet guy, so I hid my scooter behind the road sign for the hotel. Road sign probably doesn't do it justice. It was built out of towering stone, had no less than three fountains of water spewing into the air at a time, and was highlighted with striking red and blue lighting. It was safe to say my little scooter was hidden behind the fanfare.

I rushed through the hotel lobby and didn't see Kita at the elevators. I cursed myself for missing her until I spotted the smart pony tail and satchel. She headed down a grand hall that opened up into shops on either side, like an indoor mall. Most were high end but some were kitschy and touristy. I followed the paper mage without difficulty as a sparse crowd filled between us.

Instead of shopping or heading to a hotel room, she exited at the end of the hall. I peeked through the glass doors. The sun beamed down on a large pool and several hot tubs lined with beach chairs. A long bar snaked around the building wall. A patio restaurant and cabanas provided ample lounge and table seating.

Kita Mariko walked straight to the bar and ordered a frozen Piña Colada. Not exactly the essence of evil, I know, but trust me on this one. She's a ruthless bitch.

A ruthless bitch on vacation. Relaxing. And planning to be here a while by the way she was nursing her drink.

I frowned. There was plenty of activity outside, but it wasn't packed by any means. My jeans and cowboy boots would stand out like a sore thumb in this island paradise. I made my way back to the shops and found a clothing store that wasn't a complete rip-off. Five minutes later I stashed my clothes in a locker, slung a towel over my shoulder to hide my face, and made my way poolside wearing a pair of trunks and knock-off sunglasses.

A woman in a lounger wearing an oversized hat undressed me with her eyes. I guess that was easy wearing only shorts, but I realized the flaw in my plan. My entire life —my old life—I hadn't had these sculpted muscles. My physique was a product of years of slave labor, so the stares were pretty new to me. The last thing I wanted was Kita Mariko checking me out.

The second flaw stemmed from the fact that the patio tiles were searing my bare feet and I was doing an undignified two-step. That was likely to attract even more attention.

I solved both problems by easing into a hot tub. It was fitted against the pool, its wall reaching high above the water surface, a tiny waterfall pouring from its basin into the much larger pool below. The higher vantage helped hide my face as I melted into the tub. The soles of my feet thanked me.

Talk about relaxing. Alone in a ten-by-ten bubbling spring of water, a cool breeze taking the edge off the blaring sun—Kita could nurse that Piña Colada all day for all I cared.

The old Cisco Suarez would've walked right up to her and demanded satisfaction. Hell, I would've done as much *last week*. But Project: Cayman was an information-gathering operation. Blue Sky was linked to Rudi, who was linked to the Covey, who had ties to properties and businesses in the Caymans. There was an interconnected web that needed working through, and moving too fast might get me caught up in it. Better to watch the spider work from a distance.

I chilled in the hot tub longer than Kita had been in the bank. After a while, taking a nap seemed a good proposition.

A splash of water jarred my eyes open. I hadn't actually been sleeping, but I'd been close. Two women sat in the hot tub across from me, trading glances and giggling. My eyes darted to Kita. Good. She was still there. Her drink was melted now but half full. I turned to the new company with a chagrinned look and tried to ease back down naturally. Maybe I'd played it off.

"Long day?" asked one of the women. She was blonde with inviting features: buxom and short, with natural buoyancy in a bikini top, if you know what I mean. Her friend looked eerily similar despite being a natural brunette. They were both pretty, all long eyelashes and charming smiles.

"You could say that," I answered after they noticed I'd been staring. "Let me guess. Sorority sisters?"

They both smiled. "Oh my God. Barf!" exclaimed the brunette. "Just sisters. My name's Gemma and this is Jade." Jade waved and Gemma slid across the tub toward me. "She's shy," she fake confided in a fake whisper.

Jade studied the water for a moment before meeting my gaze. "I just wait until I have something useful to say instead of blabbering every thought in my head. It's not the same thing."

I nodded. Gemma giggled and slid back to her side of the pool. "What are you staring at that woman for?"

I stiffened. "What?"

"That Asian woman. Is she your wife or something?"

Kita was still blissfully oblivious so I tried to look nonplussed. "I'm not married. I don't even know her."

Gemma turned to her sister and raised her eyebrow inquisitively.

"What?" I asked.

Gemma shrugged. "Too bad. I like married men the best."

Jade dropped her jaw and splashed water at her. "Gemma! Stop it."

The brunette winked at me. "But Jade likes them single."

The poor girl couldn't meet my eyes again. I didn't blame her. Gemma, the pimp.

Jade rolled her eyes and slid away from her sister. "Don't think bad of her. She always gets this way at weddings."

I chuckled politely. "Who's getting married?"

Jade slid closer. "My best friend. Gemma and I are bridesmaids."

"And single," added Gemma.

I made a sour face. "Well, I hate weddings and I forgot to pack a tux, so don't get any ideas."

Gemma laughed it off and flung her hair over her shoulder, but she stowed the conversation. I ran my hand through my hair and tried to act like a guy who wasn't stalking political money. Eventually, the two women whispered to each other and Gemma announced she'd be back and disappeared inside the hotel.

"I hope not too soon," said her sister.

"That's no way to talk about family."

Jade shrugged. "It's not like we're besties or anything."

"Gotcha. I guess I won't hold her against you."

That had come out wrong, but it wasn't an entirely uncomfortable thought. She laughed and reverted to quiet again. I had to say, I could appreciate her serene beauty. She didn't try too hard, like her sister. But I reminded myself that it only *looked* like I was on vacation.

A few more minutes passed. I was getting all pruny in the hot tub and wondered how much longer I was gonna need to tough it out. Kita had set aside her unfinished drink by now but didn't appear ready to leave.

"You do know her, don't you?" asked Jade.

It had been obvious I was looking this time. There was some kind of connection, though. Something about Jade's face made it tough to lie outright. "It's complicated."

She bit her lip to stifle a frown. Maybe she thought I was blowing her off.

"Look, it's nothing like that. I'm just keeping an eye on things. Like a bodyguard."

Jade's eyes lit up. "That sounds more exciting than a wedding." She turned to the bar and I realized I'd said too much.

I gently spun the woman around by the shoulders. Her skin was supple and pink. "Don't look at her. You're too obvious."

"Sorry. I'd make an awful bodyguard."

I stared at her cleavage bound by a white bikini top. "You'd certainly draw a lot of attention."

She blushed and sat lower in the tub. I didn't know what to say. Jade giggled for a second and leaned closer to me. "You realize you never told me your name."

Cisco Suarez, masterful flirt. "I'm Cisco," I answered, chiding myself for having more important things to deal with. At the moment.

"That's cute," she said. Then her eyes fixed on someone in the distance and she gasped.

Without pretext, Jade plunged her head underwater in my lap. I stood awkwardly but her nails clawed into my thighs and forced me down. I searched for the source of her alarm.

Chapter 14

A group of four people dressed in business suits marched onto the patio. A South American man-and-woman team and two white guys. I knew by their dress that they were the people Kita was waiting for. A red-haired man nodded at the chief of staff as they passed before settling into a cabana with a low couch. Kita followed the group and sat with them. From my hot tub lookout, I could see half of the activity within the tent. One of the men waved at a passing waitress, who quickly attended them.

I went to slide over to the opposite side of the pool when I realized Jade was still underwater and latched onto me. I nudged her head with my hands and got a handful of blonde hair in my lap.

"I'm sorry!" chirped an old woman standing beside the hot tub. She blushed and turned away quickly as if she'd seen something going on that wasn't.

"No," I insisted. "It's not that. Come back."

She turned and scowled at me before stomping away.

She was right. What I said made it weirder. Her husband remained watching and I thought there would be trouble. Instead he met me with an approving nod. "Take your time," he said. "You don't get those forever." Then he followed his wife back to their chairs.

I wiped my face and muttered, "You've gotta be kidding me." After a deep breath, I hooked my hands under Jade's arms and yanked her to the surface. I'd expected her to be panicking and out of breath, but she just blinked at me shyly.

"What were you doing down there?" I demanded.

She scanned the patio and landed on the cabana with the secretive meeting. I saw a flash of fear in her eyes, but she fought to hide it.

"Those people," I said. "You know those people."

She lowered into the water (only up to her neck this time) and smiled weakly. "It's complicated," she said, mimicking my voice.

She had jokes. "Who are they?"

"I'd rather not get into it."

"I want to know."

She huffed and swallowed, but gave in. "I don't know really. Powerful people with a lot of money and even more friends."

"How do you know the locals? I thought you were just on vacation."

"You could say we kinda ran into them last night, and I don't want a repeat performance."

Interesting. Maybe Jade could help me after all. "What

can you tell me about them?"

She shrugged. "Not much. I don't think they're locals either, but they walk around this hotel making demands like they own everything." Her face darkened. "And *everyone.*"

I turned to the cabana. I hated them already.

The Hispanic man and woman were married, if I had to guess. Black hair surrendering to white, skin beginning to wrinkle. They spoke calmly and confidently and watched each other's backs.

The two white guys were more standoffish, not as close but perhaps partners. One was rotund and dressed more casually, in a leisure jacket and polo. He had a mane of flowing red hair with a mustache and beard, thick but trimmed. The other was thinner and balding, somewhere north of forty. He had the nicest suit of the bunch, replete with pinstripes and large cufflinks on a bright-yellow button-up.

Kita Mariko sat between both groups, not seeming to favor either side. She opened her satchel and set down a laptop, and fielded questions from everyone as she pulled up various files.

A paper mage in the digital age. I wondered if she often lamented that.

That spawned a worse thought. If Kita was an animist, like me, then what were the others? It wasn't that the Covey didn't do business with regular folk. I'd already witnessed such endeavors—Rudi Alvarez himself was a shadow puppet who didn't know the first thing about spellcraft. So I hoped that these men didn't have hidden power besides the money they exuded, but I wasn't confident.

The discussion in the cabana became animated, and the red-haired man slammed a boisterous hand on the table. Everybody shook, including Kita Mariko. Including Jade sitting beside me in the hot tub. Her nails dug into my thighs again, and I knew the red-haired man was the one who had frightened her.

"My sister must be waiting for me," she said hurriedly. "Maybe I'll see you around."

I put my hand around her waist, trying to comfort her, trying to keep her from going. "You okay?"

Her wide hips felt good in my hand, and she nuzzled closer to me in an embrace. Her lips tickled my ear and whispered, "Don't worry about me." Her voice was confident but her eyes wavered. She climbed out of the hot tub, stole my towel to hide her face, and headed inside the hotel.

"Okay then," I said to myself, trying to slow my heartbeat.

I turned my attention back to the cabana. The activity had calmed. The South Americans passed a USB key to Kita and she plugged it into her laptop. There were phone checks and handshakes. Apparently the dispute was over and it was transaction time. Unfortunately, there were no briefcases of cash for me to score. Business in the modern age. Kita Mariko finished up with the USB drive and handed it to one of the white men, but the cabana cover prevented me from seeing who.

This was curious. Wasn't it normal for Rudi Alvarez to

do the heavy lifting when it came to fund-raising? Politics were the last realm I'd claim to be an expert on, but this had all the makings of a back-door deal if I ever saw one. Then again, I'd found out the hard way that Kita Mariko was the brains of the Covey. The ghost of her own father had accused her of as much. Maybe she was the ringleader after all, working one new conspiracy after another. Part of me wanted that to be true. Then I could excuse her influence on Emily. Her own half sister had forced her to cooperate. I knew it to be true.

The meeting broke up and everyone went their separate ways. The balding man to the bar for another whiskey, neat. The South Americans returned inside and Kita Mariko followed suit. I wasn't sure who to tail but I didn't want to lose Kita again. It had been two weeks since we'd clashed—I didn't want her to vanish for another two. But then I remembered the paper trail. Evan's plea for evidence. It wasn't about *who* to follow, but *what*. The USB drive.

The red-haired man lounged in the cabana with a glass of red wine for some time more. He shuffled something in his jacket pocket. Neither him nor the man at the bar had bags or, from what I could tell, weapons. That didn't mean this would be easy, but I'd take what I could get.

With Kita gone, I was no longer concerned with being recognized, so I hopped out of the pool and retrieved another towel from the desk. When I returned, the red-haired man was still in the cabana alone, now on his phone.

I approached the bar and stood next to the balding man. "A *Cuba Libre*, please," I ordered. The bartender poured rum in a high glass. The man in the pinstripe suit didn't even glance at me. His tan hair was thinning but had strong enough comb-over skills that nobody could claim bald yet. How many more years that distinction would remain blurry was another question.

The bartender filled my glass with cola, topped it with a lime, and slid it my way. "Would you like to charge it to your room?" he asked.

"Cash." I stripped a bill from my wad and handed it to him. My cash reserves were running low but I wasn't dry just yet. I wondered what a night in a place like this would do to my balance.

I rested my back against the bar and sipped my highball, watching the man in the cabana from a closer vantage. He had a strong nose and serious eyes. I pegged him in his mid forties but not due to wrinkles or graying. He simply had the air of a man who'd been around. Maybe that meant he was dangerous.

"A last one," ordered the man in the pinstripe suit. "For the road." The bartender poured another whiskey and produced the check on request. The man walked it over to the cabana and dropped it on the coffee table. Between some murmuring, they closed the curtains of the cabana.

I didn't like it. After meeting with shady South Americans and a representative of a dirty Miami politician, why the need for privacy now? I took a swig of my drink while deciding my course of action. Fortunately, the men emerged from the cabana before I made a dumb move. Instead of heading into the hotel, though, they rounded the building corner along an outside walkway. Street access from the outside.

I was sure my cover was still intact. If Kita had seen me on her tail, she wouldn't have led me here. No one else knew who I was. Following them down that side path might be announcing myself. I wondered if they were spooked already, but shady deals require shady practices. Unexpected movements were probably standard fare with these guys.

I decided to follow in my bare feet, navigated past beach chairs and a railing, and hurried into a jog. The afternoon on the swanky patio was nice, but I was outta here.

Or so I had thought. As soon as I slipped around the corner, the balding man in the pinstripe suit was standing in my way. I jerked to a stop and peered over his shoulder, watching his partner slip away.

"Excuse me," said the well-dressed man, holding his arms to block my path.

I bet the red-haired man had the USB drive. I shoved the man in pinstripes aside to brush past him, a perk of my strong build. That was the plan, anyway, until a shockwave of lightning crackled between his fingers as they planted on my chest.

I launched backward and hit the dirt, tasting blood in my mouth. My reaction was measured, rolling away onto my knees and facing the threat, but not skippy to the idea of waging a magical battle twenty feet from fat retirees on vacation. Good thing our little path wasn't crowded.

"I'm truly sorry about that," said the man, brushing his hands on his jacket. "Think of that as a warning shot across the bow. Just to get your attention."

I clenched my jaw and rose. My attention? He was another animist. He had it.

Chapter 15

I checked behind me. No incoming ambush. Kita was still gone. There was, of course, the light crowd and patio staff. But here, in the alley along the building, it was just me and him.

"You'd better know what you're getting into, Pinstripes," I warned gruffly.

The mage smiled and adjusted the cuffs of his yellow shirt. "Simon. Simon Feigelstock, actually, but most stick to Simon."

"I don't blame them. Now about you putting your hands on me..."

Simon lifted his hands in the air. The gesture was meant to be easing, to show he held no weapons, but he and I both knew his weapons were the spirits. Which spirits exactly were anyone's guess.

I scratched my chin and considered his lightning attack. "Zeus?" I guessed. Call it professional curiosity.

He shook his head like I'd given him a report card with

all Ds. "What is it with everyone? Zeus? I mean, thousands of deities throughout human history, the literal sum of all world belief in the Intrinsics, and the best you could come up with is Zeus?" He turned away as though someone would magically appear and hear his appeal, but it was still just us.

"Don't take it personally, Simon. He was the first patron that came to mind."

"Of course he was! That's exactly my point. People don't even think to consider Ishkur the Thunderer."

I returned his gaze with a plain face.

"You know," he started. "Ancient Sumer? The Fertile Crescent? This is World History 101."

I shrugged. "I guess Mrs. Eddings glossed over the part about the Thunderer."

He smiled cheekily. "Cute. But I'll have you know Ishkur is one of the originals. He's been around the block a tad more times than Opiyelguobiran, that's for sure."

My face darkened, no magic involved. Simon knew the full name of my patron. He'd done his homework and probably knew all about me. "If you know who I am," I said carefully, "then you know getting into it right here's a bad idea."

Simon checked his comb-over. "Right you are. As I said, I just needed to get your attention. I prefer civility when possible."

I snorted. Over his shoulder and in the distance, Kita's rental car pulled along the drive and the red-haired man got in. They sped off. I should've marked her vehicle somehow.

"Say what you came here to say," I muttered.

"I respect you, Francisco."

"Cisco."

"Okay then. What you've accomplished. What you've acquired."

The Horn of Subjugation. That was the only thing he could mean. A powerful artifact capable of manipulating South Florida's voodoo community, and I had it locked in a safe.

"You have budding power," he continued. "A man of your background, I can respect that."

"Then respectfully get out of my way."

Simon chuckled nervously. He wasn't scared, however. Not that I could tell. He was simply working through how to explain something, as if speaking to a child. "You need to understand something, Cisco. What you're doing—it's bad business."

I narrowed my eyes. "Bad for who?"

"A collective of like-minded wizards."

"You've got to be kidding me. A wizard's guild?"

Simon smiled weakly. "Don't be so dramatic. We're not an ancient order of Templars or the Illuminati or anything."

"So what then? A lodge? A bunch of guys who ditch their wives so they can dress in robes and hang around a man cave trading silly rituals?"

Simon Feigelstock arched an eyebrow. "What is a man cave?"

I sighed. "Look, there is no collective of like-minded wizards. Anyone with our kind of power's a narcissist. Good luck finding a pair that agree on anything."

"Thank you for that fascinating bit of insight into the human condition." Simon rubbed the worn wrinkles on his forehead. "We are pragmatists. Businessmen with overlapping goals. We all work for ourselves, as you say, but find that aligning our efforts often yields more fruitful results. A weightier influence."

"Collective bargaining," I concluded.

"Now you've got it."

"Sounds more like a cartel to me."

Simon smiled, unfazed. "Cartels are good for business."

I furrowed my brow. Was this guy for real? I used to love reading comics, but an accurate representation of life they were not. Magic might exist, but a secret collective of wizards sounded like a bad urban fantasy novel. Corporate interests or no, it was farfetched.

"I've been around a while," I finally said. "How come I've never heard about you guys?"

He laughed off the question with a snobby guffaw. He respected me, my ass. His tone switched to full-on elitist. "We don't deal with *street-level* enforcement."

I snickered. "Fancy talk from a hired thug. The pinstripes aren't fooling anybody. You're dime-a-dozen cartel muscle, an enforcer protecting the interests of the bigger players."

The man swallowed but didn't respond immediately. That told me I'd nailed it. He stepped closer and admitted as much with a nod. "You've got it all figured out, Cisco. That means you know it's not just me you're dealing with. It's the 'bigger players' you mention that want you on board. So why don't you cut the one-man-army act and look at the big picture, huh?"

The big picture. If this painting that is my life gets any bigger it's gonna need the ceiling of the Sistine Chapel as a canvas. I gave the not-so-veiled threat appropriate consideration and frowned. "Offer declined. I don't wanna join the union."

Simon's jaw tightened. "It's not that simple."

"Why not? I saw the disdain in your eyes when you said 'street level.' I'm beneath you, so leave me alone and let me handle my business."

"You can't go around blasting prominent politicians without rubbing investors the wrong way."

City Commissioner Rudi Alvarez. I'd struck a nerve. "I didn't touch Rudi. It was a poltergeist that ripped up his front yard."

"Which is why this is only a warning," shot back Simon, coming full circle. "You want to smoke ghosts and vampires? Be my guest. But connected animists and politicians are off limits."

And there it was. Cisco Suarez had gotten too big for his britches, apparently. I nodded my head toward the street. "Is that what Redbeard is? Connected?"

Simon turned his head but saw the empty driveway. Something had him flustered. "That's what this is about?" he asked. He straightened his jacket and reclaimed a cool exterior. "And here I thought you were playing politics. That other man's a nobody. A political booster. He doesn't live here. He's only on Grand Cayman because

Commissioner Alvarez and his chief of staff are priming candidates for a big fund-raiser in Miami. There's nothing amiss here."

"You and I must have different definitions of amiss. I know about the commissioner's hidden money."

"Well, you'll just need to forget about it."

I jutted my chin out. "Or what?"

Simon almost looked bored now. "Haven't you been listening? Or the Society will get involved. There's a lot more people to deal with than me. Believe me. That's why we call it the Society."

Confident. Aloof. Professional. I had the feeling Simon was dangerous.

"Something you should know about me," I said, stretching my fingers and then balling them into a fist. "I took orders for ten years. I'm done with that. So when people tell me what to do, it leaves a bad taste in my mouth."

He sighed. "Some sort of truce, then? No one will go after the other, as long as each behaves?"

I didn't get it. If his wizard cartel was so big and powerful, why was he dealing with a small-time shadow charmer like myself? Could be that the wraith had them scared, had them unsure of what exactly the Horn of Subjugation could do. Hell, *I* was unsure of what it could do.

"What about Kita Mariko?" I asked. "She protected too?"

Simon nodded slyly. So the mysterious Covey I was hell-bent on taking down had made more friends than just politicians and businessmen. The Covey was connected to the Society too. The one percent looking out for each other. Sure sounded like a cartel to me.

I laughed at the ridiculousness of it. "I get it. The paper mage cried foul. Did she happen to mention that she was intimately involved with my death and zombie servitude? Or is ten years outside the Society's statute of limitations?"

The enforcer tilted his head as if the offense was minor. "Truthfully? It was below our radar."

"That's right," I scoffed. "I forgot. *Street level.*" If Simon wasn't trying to piss me off, he was doing a piss-poor job. "Tell me this," I said, stepping into his personal space now. "You and me. Right here, right now. This is the *street*, isn't it?"

There was a glimmer in his eye. For all his external etiquette, the man wanted to smack me down hard. I bet he looked forward to it.

Simon Feigelstock cleared his throat. "Fortunately, I don't need to get in your way. Not now. There's nowhere for you to go. Business concluded a day early. Connor and Kita are already at the airport by now."

A slight panic fluttered in my chest but I forced it down. The wizard cartel may have known about me, Simon may have gotten in my way and let the USB drive slip away, but I wasn't gonna give him the satisfaction of seeing my disappointment. Instead, I focused on the man's unintentional slip of the tongue.

"Connor?"

The enforcer worked his jaw, realizing his mistake, but said nothing.

"They headed back to Miami? To the fund-raiser you mentioned?"

Simon regained his composure and smiled. "You don't get it, Cisco. Any moment now, they'll be boarding a private jet headed to a private island. I'm done here. And so are you. The relevant parties have been warned and are beyond your reach."

The man in the pinstripe suit brushed past me to head back to the patio. My hand swiped the shadows, broke open my sawed-off shotgun to confirm it was loaded, and then snapped it closed and trained it at the back of his head. When Simon heard the click, he froze.

The Society enforcer turned to me slowly and adjusted his tie. "Put that thing away before someone gets hurt."

"That's the idea."

Impatience again. "Consider what it is you really want, Cisco. Then consider how utterly disconnected I am from it. You may not like me, but we're not enemies. Not yet, anyway."

"Just a jobber putting in the hours, are you?"

He winked at me. "Consider the truce. It's a fair offer. We could make your life difficult, but we haven't started yet. Maybe, when this all settles, we might even prosper together."

I licked at the blood still in my mouth and lowered the weapon. Simon Feigelstock smiled appreciatively and went on his way.

Whatever dirty dealings the man was into, he was right. It wasn't him that had killed me way back when. I didn't know fact one about the Society. It was an easy guess that they weren't about unicorns and rainbows, but I wasn't the spellcraft police.

Maybe one day they'd get in the way of what I wanted again. Maybe that one day was inevitable. Maybe, if it came to blows, I'd be better prepared and willing to take out Simon later.

But maybe I didn't need to deal with the wizard cartel at all. I'd never seen them in Miami before. Maybe their influence was more international. I reminded myself that I was in the Caymans only for information gathering, and I still had more to get.

I returned to the patio. Simon was gone now, just like my chance of pursuit. Kita may not have seen me tailing her, but *someone* had obviously known about me. At least now I knew about them too.

As I passed the cabana with the drawn curtains, I slipped inside. Still empty. No one had carelessly left behind a thumb drive with their evil plans on it. I wondered where that left me. Before I left I noticed the check on the table beside the empty wine glass. I couldn't make out the scribbled signature, but it kinda maybe started with a C.

Connor. Was he a booster? A connected animist? Another puppet, like Alvarez? I couldn't be sure of anything yet.

Redbeard may have been boarding a plane to a private island by now, but Simon said their business had concluded a day early. That meant everyone had planned on sticking around another night.

Whether Connor was still in town or not, I did have a new lead on a location of interest: his room number, 2417, was printed beside his signature on the check.

Chapter 16

Back in the day I had a small-time voodoo partnership, but these last few weeks (after my "hiatus") introduced me to the joys of working alone. I was a private practitioner now, through and through. Only, all of a sudden, I was deep-rooted in Miami politics, Nether curses, and under the oppressive eye of one wizard cartel.

Cheer up, Cisco. You've made it to the big time.

I was dejected. I even (briefly) considered backing down. (Momentarily.) I saw the wisdom in backing down, at least. Yup, the benefits of not directly challenging a secretive collective of animists were reeeeal convincing, right up to the point that I broke into Connor's hotel room during maid service.

Hey, what can I say? I'm an opportunist.

I pretended I owned the place, asked for extra towels, and gave the nice lady a sizable tip—oh, and I ordered plentiful room service—all charged to Room 2417. High-end crab, shoestring fries, and a couple *cervezas*. It took the edge off.

Simon the enforcer must have been telling the truth about Connor leaving town because he didn't awkwardly walk in on me taking a shower or wearing his bathrobe and slippers. It wasn't all living the high life, though. I spent most of the time exhaustively searching the room for clues. Unfortunately, I didn't find any crumpled papers in the trash with secret codes revealing his next whereabouts. I even ran a pencil over the pad of paper by the phone but, lo and behold, it turns out people don't write down messages anymore. I would've attempted the old redial trick on the hotel phone, but I realized the last call was me ordering food.

This is why I'm not a private investigator.

Luckily, I did find a spare key card for the room sitting on the nightstand in an envelope with the Wi-Fi code. Connor had probably kept one and dropped the copy here. That meant no more brushes with the cleaning crew. I wiped the fossils of room service off the bed (to the floor) and took a load off. I could get used to king-size beds and bathrobes.

Thoughts of the Society intruded on my leisure. I wasn't sure what to make of them. Having bigger players involved changed the playing field, like every other episode of Dragon Ball Z. My investigation was swerving dangerously close to cartoon territory. Laughable or not, this new collective had to be taken seriously.

I didn't doubt that the Society had dirty laundry, but that didn't mean they cared about my used boxer briefs. They had their jumbo-sized hamper and I had my pile on the floor. It wasn't much, but I had enough to worry about without sharing a load. (I bet you never heard a guy go on with a dirty laundry metaphor so long before.)

The point is, we didn't have to come to blows. But that didn't mean I bought into their claim of neutrality either. I did, however, believe that I'd been under their radar. I was the Covey's business. So why was the Society involved at all?

It was obvious why they went to bat for the paper mage. Rudi Alvarez is a prominent politician. Until now I'd assumed all the money he embezzled was for personal gain. Now I had to consider the Covey's and the Society's interests as well. What a tangled web greed weaves.

I began to see the lack of confrontation so far as a good thing. Sure, I'd backed Rudi into a corner and he'd set loose his dogs—he was still after me—but he was never calling the shots. Finding him in the Caymans wouldn't have netted me much more than I already had.

I tossed over the details in my head. It felt good to slow down, drink a beer, and investigate while I decided how to handle my larger problems.

I raided the minibar, hung a "Do Not Disturb" sign on the door knob, and smuggled a couple beers and a pack of Peanut M&Ms to the hotel office beside the downstairs lobby. Perfect, an empty room and a computer. It took some doing, but I found references to the owner of the hotel: one Connor Hatch. No pictures, but the woman from the hot tub had said that the guy acted like he owned the place. Maybe that was because he actually did.

Going off that name, I found Connor had a background in security services and was an investor in several companies. He also had strings of real estate in the Caribbean, Nicaragua, Panama, and Venezuela. I never found reference to his residence or private island ownership. If Simon was bullshitting about that, then maybe Connor was still within reach.

I didn't have much and soon ran out of ideas for searches. Maybe he *was* just a booster. A man with money. Connected.

Then I considered another name I'd been meaning to research. Henry Hoover: father of Kita Mariko and Emily Cross, world traveler and real-estate tycoon, and murder victim of Cisco Suarez. I shivered. The Covey ordered his death for a reason.

Henry's properties were now owned by his daughters. At the height of his equity, his real estate was perhaps on par with Connor's, less extravagant but spread around the world. He was Australian born and had a lot of business there and in Asia before his later years in Latin America. He developed a lot of property for housing contracts, so his influence was always shifting around. I made notes of several Grand Cayman properties, but nothing stood out. These leads would require boots on the ground.

I also did some ancillary searches on Covey members, but didn't turn up much. The former head of security (and volcanic elemental) hadn't resurfaced since being fired. There wasn't any history on him. It bugged me that he was missing, if only because I couldn't see him coming. Then there was the question of Rudi Alvarez. I had hoped to find him here but only ran into Kita.

But the politician's business did result in a hit. His new pet project, the Passport to Latin America, a business initiative with South Florida, the Caribbean, and Central and South America. A joint project to enrich trade. That was the business his office had said he was in the Caymans for. That was the business he should have been attending to. And the primary fund-raiser event was being held in Miami three days hence.

"Gotcha, Rudi," I said. It had taken a day and a half to sail here. If I left tomorrow afternoon, I'd have all morning to prepare for the event. It's not that I thought Rudi could tell me anything new, but having a private one-on-one might convince him to call off his dogs. At times I could be... persuasive.

Eventually, my beers and my mind were all dry, and I figured I'd done enough work for my first day in the Caymans. I checked the lobby and shops for familiar faces. I ordered a beer when I found the patio free of animists and wandered to the beach. Maybe it was the alcohol or the night sky (probably the alcohol), but I figured I'd earned a break. I hiked out to the sand and found a hotel chair to collapse in.

The sound of the waves worked wonders on my soul. Some magic has nothing to do with spirits and everything with being human. I sipped my beer and let the stress melt away. Vigilante justice was hard work. Too bad I didn't have time to take another day out here. You know, to "investigate leads." With the cash I saved on the hotel room, I could swing the extra expenses.

A shuffle of sand behind me jolted my eyes open. A flash of blonde hair fell over my head before two hands from behind covered my eyes.

"Guess who?" came an alluring voice.

With the blonde hair, my first thought was Emily. It wasn't logical or reasonable, but it was what my body wanted. Of course, it wasn't her and I knew it.

I let out a long breath and eased back into the chair, glad I hadn't pulled my shadow trick. "Um..." I slow played her. "Let's see. I've met so many gorgeous women in hot tubs today."

Jade laughed and uncovered my eyes, immediately going for a playful pat on my shoulders. I was wearing the tank with the trunks now, figuring for a cool breeze, but the air was warm anyway. So was Jade as she sat sideways in my lap.

Despite her voluptuous figure, she wasn't heavy at all. No sir, she could stay there all night.

"Wedding over?" I asked.

"That's not for another day," she said, lifting her arms above her head and pulling her long hair back. The resulting effect on her chest was... seductive. The thin white triangles of her bathing suit strained against her breasts, and she held the pose just long enough for me to know it was on purpose. There was something about her skin that was riveting. Pinker than I was used to in Miami and most of what I'd seen in the Caribbean. She seemed untouched by the sun.

"So how goes your complicated personal life?" she asked with a smirk.

"It doesn't seem so complicated at the moment."

"No?" She wiggled in my lap and put her arm around me. "I'm not surprised. Vacations simplify things."

I shrugged and locked my arms around her waist. Her bare skin was cool to the touch. I thought about ripping off the wrap she wore to see how the rest of her bare skin felt. She must have read my mind.

"Mr. Cisco!" she said with a mock gasp. "Behave yourself!"

"It's Suarez," I said. "And you're just gonna have to deal with fast-and-loose Cisco Suarez tonight. I've had a few beers. Believe it or not, I'm not a big partier."

She giggled and grabbed my half-empty bottle, chugging most of it.

"I guess you've had a few too."

She winked and upturned it in my mouth until it was dry. I took the empty bottle and pitched it in the sand. She was already onto rubbing my forearm tattoo.

"What's this mean?" she asked.

Oh, just an ancient Nordic power symbol that looks like an arrow, but is really just one branch of a more powerful sigil called the Helm of Awe. "I like arrows," I said, realizing I didn't have a cover story for my tattoos yet.

She nodded. "I like tattoos."

"I've got another," I said, producing my left palm. She jumped when she saw the black mark covering my hand. I did too, a little. The mark was darker than before, like a rot was setting in. It had spread to cover my entire palm, too. I told myself my skin was fine. It was just a hex. Something I needed to look into when I got back to Miami.

"Sorry," I said, closing my fist. "Forgot I burned myself." Jade's eyes widened and I could tell she wanted to ask about it. I tried to change the subject. "Do you have any tattoos?"

She smiled again and shifted in my lap, looking over her shoulders as she turned her back to me. Her lashes fluttered and she looked down, curving her back so her butt was pressed close. Message received, loud and clear. Now I really wanted to peel her wrap off. When I reached, she jumped off me and skittered away.

"You wanna do something crazy?" she asked, looking up and down the beach. The company was surprisingly sparse.

"Let's get married and get tattoos declaring our love for each other," I said.

Jade rolled her eyes. "I really need to spell it out for you, don't I?" She unwrapped the cloth at her waist and tossed it toward me. The wind carried it into my face. When I brushed it aside, Jade was racing to the ocean.

"Don't have to spell *that* out," I murmured.

I followed her with a too-cool-for-school walk, but I was really just buying time. I was a bit nervous. I'd only been the well-muscled, attractive-to-girls Cisco Suarez for three weeks, and most of that time I'd been fighting for my life. The chance to have fun, to be normal—scratch that—to be exceptional, had hardly occurred to me.

I was single. Missed most of my twenties and early thirties. My old girlfriend was married to my best friend.

Hell, I was on *vacation* in the *Caymans* on a *private beach* in a *luxury resort* with a *beautiful woman.* What was I weighing my options for? Like Jade had said, vacations simplify things.

Already knee-deep in the water, she beckoned me and walked backward. I pulled off my tank top and headed in. She hopped away playfully but I closed the distance in no time. The water fought against us as we trekked along the sandbar, chest deep. Jade giggled and laid her back against a gentle wave, but dashed further before I could reach her. Then she unhooked her bikini top. Her blonde hair was matted down by water that flowed down her shoulders and over her breasts. They bounced as she hopped furtively away. Then she sank to her neck, depriving me of the view.

I pushed ahead until we were only a few yards apart, she seductively backing away, me joining the dance. Jade's smile had a dastardly tinge to it, and she let her chest surface once more to tease me onward.

We walked deeper into the sea, pushing through gentle current, the tension building between us, before she raised her hand for me to stop. I obeyed, but my face made it clear she couldn't hold me off for long. Her eyebrows arched in pleasure.

"It's beautiful out here," she said. She was right.

Seven Mile Beach was stunning this far out. The sandbar stretched an impossible distance from the shoreline. I could see the entire curve of the island. The ocean was calm, the waves slow and steady, very conducive to what I had in mind. When the other half of Jade's swimsuit floated to the surface, I knew she agreed. I couldn't hold back anymore.

I closed in as she wrapped her arms around my shoulders. Her breasts squeezed against my chest. She pulled my mouth down into hers. We kissed, both hungry from our hunt, impossible to sate. She shook a little as the tension fled her body then pulled back and ran her hand over my chest.

"You're a good kisser," she said softly.

"I'm good at other things."

She smiled. "I almost regret having to do this." Then she yanked my head underwater with her full weight.

Bubbles rushed past my face, disorienting me. I thought she was playing rough at first, but her grip was strong. Somehow, I was upside down, the comforting sandbar out of reach.

I thrashed in the water, looking for purchase, trying to shake free. I batted her arms away and she spun around me. Between the bubbles, I caught a glimpse of a large fish body snaking after Jade, each scale as green as her namesake.

Chapter 17

Mermaids are bad business.

I'd never met any firsthand before, but the sum of their mystique centers on luring gullible men into the depths to drown. That was it. That's what they're known for. And here I was—a man, no doubt, but also a formidable animist —and I'd fallen for it, hook, line, and sinker.

Did that mean she was lying about me being a good kisser?

Jade snaked her body around me like an eel. Her cold scales kept a surprisingly firm grip around my legs, pinning them together.

Nobody's invincible—I don't care what kind of magic they sling. My first instinct in times like this is safety. The thought process is simple: Get away from the big thing with the claws. *Then* counterattack. The only problem was, I wasn't sure where to get away to. And the big thing with the claws was a small woman with a fish tail.

I tried to melt into shadow, to dash several feet away

from the constricting serpent, but my body snagged on something. I couldn't reach the darkness.

There are things that can trap me in this world. Iron can bind my magic easily. The firm grip of a creature is often enough to keep me in place. Or even when I can shift through shadow, they sometimes come with me. This time was different. My magic responded sluggishly. I wasn't trapped, but numbed somehow.

It occurred to me that I'd never tried to duck into shadow in the ocean before. Was it not possible to rematerialize within the fluid? Was the salt in the water, legendary for disrupting the Intrinsics, neutering me?

These were the things I thought about while my brain was slowly deprived of oxygen.

Despite the seeming strength of her fish parts, Jade's top half was a diminutive woman. Maybe she was stronger than she had a right to be, but I had to have her beat. I shoved her away, callused hands scraping supple flesh. It was almost like fighting a pillow, and just as frustrating.

Keeping her at arm's length wasn't going to solve the problem of her tail wrapped around my legs. Her bottom half must have doubled in length in her true form, so she had plenty of serpentine mileage to tangle me with. I figured the only way to make her let go was to hurt her.

Underwater, my punches had a dreamlike quality. Sluggish, ineffective, like a slow-motion John Woo shot, only with bubbles instead of doves. (Are bubbles a heavy-handed metaphor for anything?)

Not only were my attacks slow by days, but Jade was

alarmingly quick in her element. She effortlessly slid to and fro, frustrating every ounce of my spent effort.

I coughed my last breath of air out in a heave. My lungs burned, but I couldn't do anything for them. I kicked my legs, but that moved me up and down more than her. Except even the words "up and down" began to lose meaning. With motion in every direction possible, I grew lost and off-center. And that was before the delirium kicked in.

I pulled my chest to my knees and scratched at her green half. Her scales were tough like armor. Instead, I reached lower and caught the end of her translucent tail fin. *This* was the soft stuff.

Gripping meaty flesh in both hands, I ripped the fin apart. The skin tore easily under my power, and for the first time I felt Jade's stranglehold loosen.

The mermaid lunged at me with open jaws. My tattooed forearm met her bite. Razor-sharp teeth crunched down like a horse on a bit. Her anger was evident in her reddened eyes.

At least I didn't need to lie about the tattoo anymore.

I tugged at her Achilles Tail harder, threatening to take a piece with me. She unwrapped herself and swam away. I could've held on, but I figured she'd be going deeper. Instead I kicked off in the opposite direction.

Blinded by blue and struggling to get even my enhanced vision to help me, I paddled into the nothingness, hoping my gamble was right. I was verging on passing out when, after a few panicked seconds, my head burst free of the water. My lungs devoured the open air.

The sandbar was gone. There was no place to stand, gain purchase, or defend myself. I treaded water with violent kicks, hoping to keep unseen threats from my exposed body. My breaths came quick but heavy, trying to recover lost air but ready to hold again at a moment's notice. I spun around, trying to orient myself.

I was farther adrift than I'd thought. The city lights were a faint glow. Jade must have taken me deeper while we were under. She could've been anywhere, and I was still too far from safety.

I attempted to draw the night shadows from the surface of the water, but even those resisted me. Without the spell tokens in my belt pouch, my knife, or my command of darkness, my options were extremely limited. Swim-like-hell limited.

The water rocked below. Something swept past me. A couple times, with a gulp of air, I submerged myself to look back and forth. Jade wasn't around. I needed to see if anything else was.

In the open air again, I let the black leak into my eyes, enhancing my night vision. The only nearby object was a plastic grocery bag. Littering assholes, but they gave me an idea.

My spellcraft was limited, and it wasn't Jade's doing. The saltwater theory was sounding real good. Maybe I wasn't able to draw shadow off the water itself, but that plastic, small as it was, was a different beast. I swam toward the bag just as something raked my stomach.

I spun and kicked, but too late. My foot whiffed through

the water. My blood floated to the surface, now inert from the extra salt. Jade was still here, and she was on the attack.

She came again. I blocked the blow with my arm and she jetted past. I turned around and predicted her next attack vector. This time, she caught me in the stomach again, but I clamped my legs around her and held her away from me.

At the same time, I pulled at the string of darkness, leading a small line off the bag and snagging it on Jade's head. I tugged the magic, jerking her head backward. You might think she could easily pull the bag with her, but shadow is of the ether. It's not a physical thing attached to this world, to that object. Moving the bag moved the source of the shadow, but pulling the shadow didn't move the bag.

Jade shrieked at me and fought the pull like a big catch struggling on the line. But the meager shadow on the grocery bag wasn't strong enough. The mermaid ripped her head away, leaving strands of blonde hair in my magical grasp and me in her wake.

Twenty feet past, she screamed in rage. She charged me on the surface of the water now. Flashbacks from *Jaws* played through my head, except I wasn't equipped with a rifle or explosive oxygen tank, only a plastic bag. I was gonna need a bigger boat.

I yanked the shadow around to catch her again, but I couldn't coax it long enough and she was too fast. The mermaid crashed into me and we both sped along the water. I inhaled what could be my last breath before we went under. At least I'd made it a big one.

Her jaws nipped at my stomach as a mass of blonde hair

covered my face. I pushed away her snapping teeth as much as I could. That, combined with my magically thick skin, allowed me to avoid serious damage. But that wasn't Jade's real play.

If I was a wide receiver, she was a linebacker, wrapping me up and taking me down. Only we wouldn't be bouncing on the turf, getting up, and slapping each other's butts in a show of sportsmanship. This was a long and slow tackle, and we were sinking deeper and deeper into oblivion.

I kneed her bare stomach, but I couldn't get enough force behind it. I clawed at her back with negligible results. As the bubbles escaped my mouth and the timer left on my oxygen ticked down, I'm not ashamed to say I resorted to pulling hair.

I'm not talking a wimpy shadow thread gripping a tuft of blonde, either. This was two strong man-fists fully wrapped to her scalp. I jerked her head back and she writhed in pain. Her eyes narrowed to vindictive slits. I shrugged and yanked her head even more, forcing the mermaid to arch her back and alter course. Instead of diving deeper, we leveled out.

Two dainty hands clasped my throat and squeezed. The constriction forced half my air out in a panicked gasp before I released her and clawed at my neck. I overpowered her and pulled her hands away, but the damage was done. She darted away and swam to my flank, just far enough that I could still see her.

I spun with the mermaid, expecting her charge, but ripped tailfins and torn hair had taught Jade the value of patience. She stayed back, watching me with eager eyes, circling me like a shark. Or rather, a vulture. Why fight when she could simply wait for me to die?

At least I wasn't disoriented anymore. I knew where up was, even if I couldn't see the sky. After another agonizing moment of staying ready, I knew it was make-or-break time. I coiled like a spring and kicked up, shooting toward the surface.

My hands thrust at my sides. I kicked my legs wide as Jade reached out for me. For one focused moment I swore I could make it, but trying to outrace a mermaid underwater is like grappling a minotaur. It's not done.

While my arms were at my side, Jade suddenly clamped me from behind in a bear hug. I tried to push away as her serpent tail wrapped up my legs, locking them together again. With a heaving motion, she pulled her locked fists into my stomach. It was the Heimlich maneuver, except it hurt like a bitch because she pressed against my wounded abdomen. The little remaining breath in my lungs came gurgling out.

I choked back the water that filled my lungs. I flopped around like a salmon in the jaws of a bear, feeling outclassed and overexerted. For all my frantic struggling, I barely managed to spin in her grasp so her chin was planted in my chest.

We stared eye to eye, and I could feel the life leaving me. My head lightened and everything became fuzzy. Comfortable almost. My muscles relaxed so much that Jade loosened her grip and pulled away, still entwining my legs but tracing my jawline with her fingers.

My God. I stared at her weightless breasts and firm, pink nipples and thought this wasn't the worst way to die. It took effort to keep my eyes open. More and more, I just wanted to lean into her welcoming grasp and go to sleep.

My teeth clamped down on my tongue to shock myself awake. The pain was sharp—the complete opposite of everything else my body was feeling. It was enough to alert my instincts to danger again. I grew panicked, alarmed, but I was still too weak to fight her off.

Jade smiled at my defiance. As she had done on the beach chair, she lifted her hands over her head and tamed the strands of blonde hair that floated in all directions. She pulled the hair over her shoulders seductively. I remembered Emily doing that.

My hand reached for her face, but Jade grabbed my wrist tightly. She stuck her lips out in a flirty pout that was half sad for me, and she brushed my hand against her hardened nipple. Then she leaned in for one last kiss.

The taste of blood wandered through my senses, and I remembered my feeble attempt to fight the delirium. Once again I bit down, skewering the tip of my tongue open. The pain was less therapeutic now, less intense. Even my ability to hurt was slowly fading. But the blood rushed freely in my mouth now, and that's the last thing you want to arm a necromancer with.

Jade wrapped her full lips around mine and I spit hot fire down her throat. She tried to draw back but I held her close, wrapping my forearms together, giving her the kiss she wanted.

I was too weak to hold it. She bucked out of my grip and darted haphazardly around. I couldn't focus on that. A lazy motion was all I could manage, but I pushed for the surface. It was a slog—ten seconds that lasted ten years—but I'd been through a decade of pain before. Every thrust built my confidence and strength, my body lying to itself about how dead I was, the biological equivalent of closing your eyes and covering your ears and shouting, "Nah, nah, nah. I'm not listening." And when I broke the surface and breathed in new life, my body burned with a fire that wanted to live. I wasn't going to die in this ocean.

Jade thrashed in the water underneath. I'd hurt her bad. No one wants black magic eating their insides, and she'd opened the door most vulnerable. So I was stunned that she clawed me from below, refusing to call off the attack.

I pushed off her with my feet, shooting away and buying time to hoard air in my lungs. The plastic grocery bag caught on my shoulder as I created distance between us. Jade's head popped out of the water twenty feet from me, and she was still gagging from my voodoo.

"What do you think of my kisses now?" I asked.

She hissed and charged me again, her tail splashing in and out of the water.

If she was determined to have this end in death, I'd oblige her.

She wrapped me up in a football tackle again. Instead of fighting her, I caught the plastic grocery bag, wrapped it around her head, and pulled it tight against her neck. She kept us shooting across the surface of the water like we were on skis, but she couldn't outrun her need to breathe.

Jade tried to wriggle away from me as she had done many times before, but this time *I* locked onto her. My legs clamped around her body and I fought off her arms with my elbows. She spun me around a few times like a gator, but I held tight.

Finally, in a last ditch effort, she dove under the sea.

Her swimming grew erratic, her resistance less focused. Her arms stopped clawing at me. Suffocating someone is a primal, personal thing. Every part of me wanted to stop, to keep myself from crossing an unspoken line. She jerked and convulsed in my grasp. I stared at her jade scales, trying to forget the human part of what I was killing.

Chapter 18

More than swimming, I floated to the shore. It was a hesitant struggle. Even over the sandbar, I was content to let the current guide me like a jellyfish as my limbs hung limply beneath.

When I finally hit solid ground, it felt foreign. The world no longer swayed and pulled at me. I used my last remaining strength to crawl to dry sand before collapsing on the beach. I'm not sure how long I lay there but the beach stayed empty for hours. When my body once again responded to my brain's commands, I started slowly by sitting up. I didn't want to push things.

My head spun and I had the beginnings of a hangover, but the night sky refreshed me. I could feel the shadow hugging me, responding to my touch. I dragged myself to my tank top and stretched it over my head, taking one last look at the ocean that had nearly claimed me.

A mass huddled at the edge of the water. It was Jade's body, already bloated and blackened. Gone were her locks of golden hair. Many of her scales had fallen away, and her skin had turned a dull gray. The stinking flesh looked more like a badly rotted manatee than anything else, and in a few hours it probably wouldn't be identifiable as even that. Fae bodies don't desiccate as much as melt.

I turned away from the monster. She'd been a pro, playing me to perfection. Gemma and Jade, the assassin sisters. I wondered if Connor sent them after me. Or perhaps the wizard cartel, breaking their truce. I didn't like either possibility. It meant they'd known about me before I ever stepped on the island.

The Caribbean had suddenly lost its charm. I was a stranger in a strange land, and if it were up to me I'd hop on a boat right now and head back to Miami. But I wouldn't see Carla until midday, and arranging alternate transportation was more trouble than it was worth. As long as I watched out for Gemma and stayed away from the ocean, I'd be fine, right?

I trudged back to the hotel room, making sure no one followed me. Inside, I wedged the desk against the door. That was about as far as I got before passing out on top of the bedsheets.

The next morning, I fixed all my problems with bacon, eggs, and three shots of espresso, delivered to my door. I fitted back into my jeans, shoes, and belt pouch. I left the room before checkout time, picked up my scooter, and hit the road.

I passed by several of the properties I'd dug up in the computer office the day before. A couple of warehouses on the south side of the island and a residence in George Town, all owned by the daughters of Herbert Hoover. Connor Hatch owned another hotel, but I was most interested with the final address on my list: a private hangar at the airport. That backed up Simon Feigelstock's claim of the personal jet. I was in no mood for a fight so I didn't snoop at any of the addresses too much, but I did confirm there was no plane in Connor's hangar.

Before the morning waned, I headed to Rum Point Beach and visited Wallace Sightseeing again. This time the little shack had lights on, the sign wasn't in the window, and the door wasn't locked.

A black man lounging on a sofa with his feet on a wicker chair pulled his attention away from the television. "We're closed for the rest of the day," he said. It was hard not to notice the bottle of Jack in his hand.

"Isn't it a little early?" I asked.

He shrugged. "It's too late to head out. What do you need?"

He spoke with a British lilt. I made him for a native Caymanian. I approached and offered my hand, but he just nodded.

"You Captain Wallace?"

"That's me." He turned his head back to the TV. "You the fishing or snorkeling type?"

I pulled a second wicker chair in front of the flat screen and sat, causing him to frown. "I just need a few minutes of your time."

He reached around me with the remote and muted the

TV, but made sure to show me he was annoyed.

"I heard you were friendly," I said.

He blinked at me.

"And talkative."

When he still didn't say anything, I decided the direct approach would be best.

"Look, Captain Wallace, I need to ask you about Stingray Tours. I don't want you to lie to me or brush me off. I don't want you to be scared. You're not in danger, and when you tell me what you know, I'm gonna stand up, walk out that door, and you'll never see me again."

Somewhere in the middle of my speech the man had stopped breathing. His eyes made like a frightened rabbit, and I knew immediately he could help me.

"What?" he asked, panicked. "I don't—"

I threw up my hand to stop him. "Captain, I'm serious about what I said. I already know the broad strokes. I know you captained tours for a husband and wife team. I know he killed himself and his wife several years back and the company went out of business. I also know that one of the company boats, the *Risky Proposition*, was stolen and used in a crime in Miami Beach."

Captain Wallace watched my lips to make sure he was hearing me right. "What crime?" he asked hesitantly.

"The murder of a man."

The man blinked then downed a couple fingers of whiskey. When the bottle again rested at his side, his eyes were glazed over. "Charles was no suicide," he said. "He and his wife were killed."

"By who?"

A nervous glance. "His boss."

"I thought Charles was the owner."

A wrinkle creased the captain's forehead. "You're not with the Royal Police, are you?"

The RCP, or Royal Cayman Police. Remember: British territory. "Do I look like I am?"

He shook his head and took another swig. "You don't see what this is? Charles owned the company, but he was in hock to drug dealers. I knew about it but didn't touch the stuff. Charles let me run the legitimate side of the business while he handled the paychecks under the table. Somehow, their partnership went south, and he was killed."

"What did he do? Transport drugs?"

"Among other things. You have to understand—that business requires a lot of coordination. People, properties, muscle. You need offices and storage space."

Suddenly I understood the value of Henry Hoover's Caribbean properties. "So drugs are moving through the Caymans."

"Sometimes, maybe, but it's mostly money. At least it used to be. Things changed around here, you know? You're American, aren't you? Your government took notice. A lot of the scams were choked out. You look up and down the street, and for every top-end sports car you see, there are ten people ready to steal it."

"You're saying business dried up?"

"I don't know," he answered, exasperated. "I got out of it a long time ago. I was never in it. That's not my life anymore. But those guys, they always find a way."

"What guys?" I asked firmly.

Captain Wallace hesitated and shook his head. "The drug dealers."

"Be more specific."

The man shivered. "They'll kill me. Just like they killed Charles and his wife. Just like whoever it was you told me about in Miami, and countless others. Why should I tell you anything?"

I stood up from the chair and leaned over him. "Because *I'm* the man that was murdered in Miami."

The captain's eyes froze and he stiffened, not doubting my words even for a second. "Hatch," he whispered.

I pulled back. "Connor Hatch?"

"Shh," he said. "Don't say that name out loud." He leaned to look out the front door to see if anyone could overhear. When he confirmed we were alone, he gave a quick nod.

It made sense. The properties scattered over the Caribbean and Central and South America. The clout with the Society. Even the ties to a corrupt Miami politician.

"Have you ever heard of the Covey? Kita Mariko? A scary Nigerian named Tunji Malu?"

Captain Wallace emphatically shook his head. "No. I never dealt with anybody."

"Tell me about Connor, then."

Liquid courage from the bottle helped him continue. "I don't know anything specific. Only stories. Only that if he knew we were speaking his name, he would have us both killed. This man... he's untouchable in these parts. He has a private army. His own island compound. He buys off governments and police. He's not just rich, he's fuck-you rich, and anything he desires he'll find a way to get. If you know what's good for you, you'll stop asking about him and leave this island."

My knees shook at the description. I chalked it up to still being weak from the midnight swim. Simon Feigelstock had told me Connor Hatch was a nobody, a booster. Only that was distantly far from the truth. Connor Hatch was Pablo fucking Escobar, and I was piggybacking off his room service.

A loud report outside made us both jump. I scrambled to the window. A man rode by on an ancient motorcycle, its mufflers periodically backfiring. I relaxed and cursed myself for getting so worked up. Stories will do that. When I turned around, Captain Wallace was holding a gun on me.

I lifted my hands slowly. "Put down the piece," I urged. "I wasn't lying about anything. I'm not here for you."

"Get out of here!" he cried. "Get as far away from me as you can!"

I could see the fear in his eyes, as if the boogeyman he'd been hiding from all these years might've finally found him. I couldn't blame his caution or his agitation. And frankly, the last thing I wanted to do was get him killed.

I eased out of his shack and backed up to my bike. Captain Wallace kept his gun on me without leaving the safety of the doorway.

"I don't want to see you again," he warned. "If I do, I'll

pull the trigger. You won't even see it coming."

"I believe you," I said and started my bike. As I pulled away, my heart was beating a hundred times a minute. The drive back to George Town was a blur of events going through my head.

Connor Hatch was a drug kingpin. Another cocaine cowboy, buying his influence one country at a time. That explained the focus on real estate to move, ship, and store product. It explained the high-rolling accounts in the Caymans. It even explained the link to Rudi Alvarez. The Miami politician could buy favors and control the flow of product to the US. Hell, with the kind of resources and connections Captain Wallace mentioned, Connor could put a dent in all competition, making it look like the US was winning the war on drugs while ever more flowed into the country.

The Passport to Latin America was fucking right.

I hurried to the port and dropped my scooter off at the rental office. Between the mermaid encounter, being muscled by the Society, and uncovering a drug kingpin as my enemy, I was starting to feel like Miami would be a bit safer than the islands. At least there all I had to deal with was a personalized SWAT team with my name on it.

Carla waited for me on the dock even though we hadn't set an exact time. I stormed past her and onto the boat without a word. She got the hint and cast off as soon as possible.

"Find what you were looking for?" she asked after a time.

"I found a lot more than that."

She grunted as if she understood. And maybe she did. But she knew better than to ask details. We avoided eye contact, looking far ahead to the expansive sky. "There's a storm coming," she said matter-of-factly.

"I'm going below deck for a while," I said. She shrugged. Before I hit the steps, I turned back to her. "Carla, can you do me a favor?"

"What's that?"

"Keep an eye out for mermaids."

Chapter 19

When Carla had warned a storm was coming, I thought she was speaking metaphorically. You know, like a contemplative scene in a movie where the good guys realize everything's about to go south.

Nope. Turns out she meant an actual rainstorm.

The *Now You See Me* wasn't harried by uninvited silvans, but the storm sure hit us full force. It wasn't a hurricane or anything—trust me, this area of the world knows how bad wind and rain can get—but the Caribbean waves finally lived up to their choppy reputation. I was too focused to get seasick, but a deeper fear pervaded my gut. We were going to be late. The delay would eat up my half-day head start.

Hey, if I didn't cut things close, you'd think less of me.

It was a hard night. The sun broke through the clouds the next morning and gave us some relief. Carla hit the motors as hard as she dared. Good for me she was fearless. We made Key Largo with little time to spare. I was squared up with Carla already (she takes full payment in advance) so

I thanked her for her skills and ran to my truck.

With some light speeding and fortuitous traffic, I could actually get to the fund-raiser before it ended. Late, yes, but in attendance. I slipped the key in the ignition and was greeted with an empty click.

"You've got to be kidding me."

I worked the starter several times. Fast key-turn repetitions, pounding the steering wheel, waiting a minute and trying to surprise it—my slew of mechanically sound tactics failed me. After I took a breath and thought about it, I realized the old pickup wasn't getting any electricity. My battery was bad.

I furrowed my brow. Except I'd just had the mechanic put in a super heavy-duty weather-guard model, precharged and ready to go. I wasn't dealing with a dead battery—I was dealing with a dead body. Or a presence, at least.

My boots stomped the gravel as I circled the front of the cab and lifted the hood. The battery was there, fresh grease on the terminals, good as new. Hell, it *was* new.

I let my pupils overtake my eyes, feeling out the shadows with my dark vision, looking for signs of a spirit. It wasn't as straightforward as it sounds, though.

Ghosts aren't the glowing phantasms you see in overexposed photographs or CGI. Spirits live in the Murk, a sort of mirror world of ours where the dead temporarily reside until they meet destiny. It's unlikely, but some manage to cross back to our side and inhabit physical objects. We call these poltergeists. I can't see them, exactly, but I can sometimes sense a signature on the objects themselves. So I could see that the car battery, to put it in the technical supernatural parlance, had been jacked up.

I leaned into the engine and whispered, "Listen up, you little gangbanger ghost. You don't like me and I don't like you, and maybe you have good reason. I killed you. But you tried to kill me too, so as far as I'm concerned, we're even. So cut this shit out with the battery and let me get to where I'm going or I'll send you back to the Murk. You hear me?"

I waited, but nothing answered.

I sighed and reached into my belt pouch. This particular spirit was stubborn. I'd opted to drive around the last two weeks rather than expel him, but it wasn't for lack of trying. For whatever reason, the usual extermination tricks didn't work. Strange, because the ghost was already defeated. By all accounts he should've retreated to the Murk and given up, but he was sticking to his guns. Luckily, he was declawed. The poltergeist could do little more than turn my wipers on unexpectedly.

But once in a while he became a real pain in the butt.

I withdrew a small mirror from half of a compact. (Yes, Cisco Suarez carries makeup products. No, he doesn't show them around.) The sun was already setting, but the sharp angle of light was a plus at the moment. I held the mirror so the beam reflected onto the battery as I spoke a word of power. Opiyel commands the shadows but also guides the dead. Think of me as an undead guidance counselor on retainer.

There was a small sizzling from the center of the battery and my engine ticked a few times, like it might when it cools after shutting off. I pulled the mirror away and nodded. "Thought you'd see it that way."

This time, when I climbed into the seat and turned the key, the sound of a healthy V8 greeted me. If only all my problems were that simple. It wasn't a coincidence that I was staring at Emily's photograph on the sun visor as I thought that. I slammed it to the ceiling and out of sight. Emily was far from simple, but photographs I could handle.

US 1 was flush with cars but we all moved efficiently. A line of ants with single-minded focus. The evening was in full swing by the time I made it to Coral Gables but I ran into no more detours. I parked in the open lot and strolled the perimeter.

The Biltmore Hotel is an old, fancy place. Distinguished is a good word. It's the type of hotel that presidents stay in when they visit Miami. Surrounded by the lush trees of a quiet Gables neighborhood, it towers over the canopy and makes you wonder who thought to put a hotel there. But that's part of the beauty.

I hated the idea of going in blind, but I was already late. There was no time to prep. At this point in the week, I was about done with information gathering anyway. If I didn't take action soon, someone else would take it for me. Again.

As I entered the old building, I glanced at the Spanish tower looming above. There were ghosts there. Like I said, you can't see them. (Not unless they're a necromancer-turned-wraith bound to a Spanish powder horn, anyway.) It was a sense, more than anything. Call it the confidence of experience.

You see, the sprawling pool and Mediterranean architecture aside, the Biltmore served as a hospital in World War II. It had seen its fair share of blood. I just hoped to avoid some of that tonight.

150

Chapter 20

The Biltmore isn't Fort Knox. It's a luxury hotel. Extravagant, inviting, and full of strangers. As such, I had free roam of the place without bother. I wandered under hand-painted ceilings and intricate chandeliers, ignoring the glitz because I knew the world was a dirtier place than it let on. Soon enough, I found what I was looking for. It wasn't hard. I just had to listen for the corny jokes and duplicitous laughter.

My destination turned out to be the Granada Ballroom, a large banquet hall that looks like a Catholic church. Stone columns set off hallways along both sides while tables set with champagne and linen consumed the inner space. It all drew the eye to a grand backdrop of ornate windows overlooking a garden.

So this was where wannabe mayors impressed people.

Applause washed through the crowd as I entered, pleased supporters all with their backs to me. With more preparation I could've worn a straw mask to cover my face.

Spun an illusion with shadow. But this was a seat-of-my-pants operation. No premeditation in sight.

I pulled the shadow over my face. It wasn't a surefire disguise, but hopefully the ballroom had more interesting things to look at than me.

Strolling in casually was the easy part. Events like this aren't locked, but they are watched. I kept my head down and moved to the outside wall, passing a huddle of security personnel. Acting like you belong is ninety percent of the work, right? Unfortunately, my scuffed jeans and sweaty tank top didn't scream high society. A large Viking-looking fellow peeled away from his detachment and followed me.

"Excuse me, sir," he called over the dying applause.

I continued moving in feigned ignorance, but that was just to buy time. Ten seconds in and the jig was already up. Oh well. I would have to earn my disguise the old-fashioned way.

This wasn't a nightclub where small infractions might be met with violence but, despite the large gentleman's manners, I knew he had a mean streak. I calmly walked under the cathedral archway of the outer hall and smiled.

This area was set off, empty like the walkways of a theater, with hanging lanterns providing dim mood lighting. The decorator did a hell of a job. The orange lights accentuated every sculpted column and every fold in the wall-length curtains. It was a stunning effect.

I huddled into the dark corner, where it was blackest, and doubled over into the wall.

"Excuse me, sir. Are you okay?"

I waited until I felt the hand on my shoulder, and then I drew the shadows around us deeply. Anybody ten feet away would have a hard time noticing us. I grabbed the security guard's hand, twisted around, and locked my arm around his neck.

I squeezed, flashbacks of Jade filling my head, but I released the man as soon as he was asleep. It was the type of up-close-and-personal deed that was dirtier than it sounded, and doing it made me wish my spellcraft extended to sleep charms.

Still under the guise of shadow, I dragged the man behind a curtain. I was lucky. This wall ran along a darkened yard; there was nothing outside the window. In the small rounded nook between the window and the curtain, nobody would see us.

I felt foolish unbuttoning the pants of a sleeping man, but it needed to be done. I wore his jacket over my tank and pulled his pants over my jeans. Everything was still so oversized I had to fold the arms and legs at the cuffs. I felt like a child wearing his father's clothes, but at least I didn't stick out so much.

I emerged from the thick curtain buttoning my jacket, checking up and down the hall and into the main room. Nobody cared about Cisco Suarez. Under normal circumstances I would've been offended.

Keeping a subtle shadow over my face, I took slow steps up the hall from column to column, scanning the well-off men and women sitting around tables pawing fancy glassware. They were toasting the speaker, who happened to be one Miami City Commissioner Rudi Alvarez.

"It is a real honor," he said with a dramatic flair, "to see each and every one of you here, supporting something we all believe in."

I rolled my eyes. Two seconds of politics was too much for me, but the crowd was eating it up. Every word out of Rudi's mouth drew more smiles. I paused to watch him work. He told a story about his father coming to America. A lot of Cubans had similar stories. Rudi got a few laughs from dad jokes, not especially funny but told in earnest. He was a good speaker. A good charlatan. A good little puppet.

"One day," he said proudly, "we will look back and know that the Passport to Latin America revitalized this city."

"Revitalized the drug business," I muttered. I couldn't believe these saps. I felt like screaming out, interrupting his eloquent speech and outing him for the lying, cheating bastard he was, right in front of his donors.

But without evidence, nobody would listen. I'd just be the crazy, anti-establishment homeless guy.

Down the center aisle, Lieutenant Evan Cross and Sergeant Ronaldo Garcia approached the stage and split off to either end of it.

Crap. Evan's team often ran personal security for the muckety-mucks. I should've counted on him being here. I had to assume the entire DROP team was running a protection detail. I realized the man I had dispatched was only a greeter, not the meat of the security. So much for easy.

How had my best friend and I gotten on opposite sides

of this? Rudi did business with the people involved in my murder, for Pete's sake. I needed to get to Evan alone. Talk to him and convince him I was in the right. He'd bluster and put his hands on his hips and boss me around in his usual cop bravado, but he was a good guy. He'd understand the situation.

I inched closer to the stage, careful not to draw my friend's eyes. I scanned the VIP tables for other threats and familiar faces, and I found one. Son of a bitch. Front and center was Connor Hatch. In the country. Must be nice to have a private jet. Here I'd been two days at sea, and Connor probably didn't have enough time to finish his beer before landing in Miami. I wondered if him being here meant the stuff about the private island was BS.

Thinking of Simon, I searched the audience again. I didn't see him, but that didn't mean the Society wasn't in attendance. This crowd was rife with hotshots who could buy the law. Something about Simon Feigelstock told me his people were of the same stock.

As before, Connor was dressed nicely, but everything from his wavy red hair to his slightly overgrown beard and his suit was just a little too casual compared to the others. That told me he was rich enough and powerful enough to not care. His prominent position in the room confirmed his place among Rudi's boosters as well.

Evan broke off from the stage and headed into the hallway on the other side of the room. As he made his way to the back, I followed on my side. If I could reach him away from the action, we'd have time to talk.

I increased my pace and marched around the back of the room to beat him to the corner, but stopped short when I saw him lean into a table at the back and kiss a beautiful blonde woman.

It was my ex, Emily.

Chapter 21

I'd had a few weeks now to get used to the idea that Emily was married to Evan. I even accepted it. What had me jittery was the thought of dealing with her betrayal. After discovering she was somehow involved with the Covey, I'd kinda shut down that part of the investigation, choosing to follow politics over Emily. It was easier to confront arcane creatures than my old flame.

But Emily was irrevocably tied to this. Her connection to Kita was what had gotten Evan his political appointment to begin with. Emily, more than anybody else alive today, made me doubt my actions the most. It's not that I wasn't right. But if I kept butting heads with the people I loved, how would things end?

Before I snapped out of my funk, Evan cleared away from the table and positioned himself by the front stage again. It had just been a quick hello to his wife, and now she sat beside the empty chair that was his. I'd missed my chance. But I could take another.

I sat down. "Hi, Em."

She spun around, face frozen in shock. Her hair was straight and rested on her bare shoulders. I'd seen another blonde up-close-and-personal recently, but Emily was all sophisticated class. Long earrings accentuated her thin neck and made her seem fragile, but I knew better. Emily was strong and had an admirable hard-to-get quality. It was what had attracted me to her in the first place.

"You can say something," I said. "I'm easy to talk to."

She frowned. The last time we had a private talk, in her kitchen, she admitted to playing me for a fool, making me fall in love with her, and bread-crumbing my way to discovering a deadly necromantic artifact. The fairer sex, I tell ya.

"You were always easy to talk to," she admitted with a soft spot in her voice. I didn't know if she was playing me again, but damn she could be convincing. "You shouldn't be here."

"Neither should you, Em. The commissioner's not a man people are gonna want to be associated with."

Her laugh was a light tickle in the air. "So Evan has said."

I nodded toward him at the stage. "What's he doing up there? He has the DROP team. He should be taking a load off and enjoying champagne with you."

"He takes his job seriously. He knows there are people like you around."

I put my hand to my heart like it was wounded. It was a

joke, but the truth was it would never heal.

"How's Fran?" I asked.

Emily thought for a minute and stared at her empty dessert plate. "She's happy."

I leaned back in the chair. I didn't know if two better words could've been said about my estranged daughter. I didn't know how to be a father—I'd never acted as one—but something paternal in me knew that, if I could hear those two words every day for the rest of my life, nothing else mattered.

"Have you thought about letting me see her?"

"Cisco... After everything—"

"Look," I cut in, drawing the eye of an older woman a couple chairs down. I lowered my voice and leaned toward Emily. "Whatever you've done to me, you must've had your reasons. That's not an excuse, but I know you weren't there. I know you weren't *directly* responsible for my death. So you played me, but you didn't kill me. In some twisted way, that means the world to me."

She took a heavy breath as I spoke.

"We don't have to love each other anymore, Em. We don't have to even like each other. But I'm not going to come after you. You're the mother of my daughter. My best friend's wife."

Now the old woman was flat-out staring. I met her eyes and glared until she looked away. Then I turned back to Emily.

After a minute she still didn't open up. "Is your sister here?" I asked, changing the subject.

She turned away. I didn't really expect her to answer. Unlike Emily, Kita Mariko had come at me hard and strong. The paper mage was only avoiding me now because I'd proven to be a formidable rival.

Watching my ex clam up, I noticed a metal locket around her neck. A heart. I knew she wasn't mine anymore —I understood that—but seeing keepsakes, personal treasures from someone else's life that couldn't be mine, pulled my heartstrings.

I fell solemn, doing my best to say what I came to say without fucking everything up again. "Emily, I'm giving you a chance to get away from the darkness."

"The darkness is attracted to you like flies to light, Cisco."

I winced. She wasn't wrong. And I was quickly losing confidence in my approach.

"I need to talk to Evan," I said. "Away from the crowd. Tell him about what I've found. I want you both on the right side of this. I don't want anything to hurt Fran."

A familiar glint sparkled in Emily's eye, a kindness in her that I'd known to be good and true at one time. "What do you want?" she relented.

I smiled, and for that second I lived in a world where Emily and I were on the same team. It was just a second, but it felt good.

My happiness was diminished when I noticed Evan's sergeant pulling a distressed greeter from behind the curtain. If this were a video game, the guard would've had the decency to stay unconscious until I cleared the level. As it was, he was out for longer than normal in real life. Garcia motioned for another man to assist him.

I sat up straight and considered my options. Ideally I could get hard evidence while everybody was around. Splash it in the faces of Rudi's hard-earned boosters. Some of them were dirty, I was sure, but for every criminal in here there was a saint who'd be horrified at what Rudi had done. Money didn't discriminate. There were good people here with the clout to do something about what I knew. At the very least, the egg on Rudi's face should put him on the defensive.

"Talk to Evan," I told her as I stood. "Tell him to meet me on the patio. Only him."

"Cisco..."

"Just do it." I hurried away from the table as Sergeant Garcia swept by. With a tug of the shadow, I slipped out the patio door.

I was lucky. The courtyard was an events space all its own, but nobody was renting it tonight. The walkway and fountain were lit for the ambiance, but the mass of the yard was dark. I squeezed into the bushes along the wall of the Granada Ballroom and peeked through the window. The curtains limited my view but I got the broad strokes.

Two DROP team members posing as guests came out of the woodwork, following Ronaldo Garcia's lead. Strangely, Evan Cross remained by the stage. At first I thought he chose to stay on the commissioner, but his pose was too relaxed. He was still smiling from the kiss with his wife. That meant Sergeant Garcia was running his own op. Could be he didn't trust Evan to capture me anymore. Could be he was right.

For their part, the police were discreet. Rudi Alvarez wasn't speaking anymore and he sat by the stage without a care. The crowd clapped as a female violinist commandeered the mic. A few shy words were her only introduction before the most beautiful piece of classical music I'd heard took over. The Granada Ballroom was enraptured while Garcia and his men searched for an interloper.

I shifted my angle and saw Emily in her seat, typing in her phone. Good. She realized how urgent the situation was becoming and was doing as I asked. After she returned the phone to her purse, I shifted back to my original position and watched Evan.

The music was loud enough to hear outside. Unfortunately, that meant Evan couldn't hear his notification. Was I seriously gonna run out of time because he forgot to set his phone to vibrate?

The sergeant finished scanning the tables and had his men check the outer halls. That included window checks, and I jumped to the side as one of the officers shone a flashlight through my window.

I took a few breaths and waited for the beam of light to turn off. Then I slowly leaned in to check the crowd.

Connor Hatch was checking his phone. His sharp features went alert as he glanced around. The red-haired man excused himself and marched down the aisle, exiting out the back of the room. The entire time, Evan stood blissfully unaware, and it sickened me to realize why he hadn't received a text.

Emily had just sold me out.

Chapter 22

Eager to avoid the ballroom but get back inside the hotel, I rushed along the center of the courtyard toward double doors that connected to the lobby. A flashlight beam flicked on and I fell backward, skidding on my feet and falling into the darkness.

My spellcraft would fizzle if the beam shone directly on me, but the police weren't looking for slithers in shadows.

When the light went away, I broke out into a run. Damn. The doors were locked. Through the glass, I saw Connor heading toward the elevators. I cursed and checked for another door. The courtyard was set between two ballrooms. Both were in use, but only one of them had police officers with weapons.

I entered door number two. A white wedding, and not a large enough affair for my intrusion to be inconspicuous. I crawled over the dessert table, apologizing profusely, and bolted for the doors to the lobby. I turned the corner and made for the elevators.

The back of Connor's suit disappeared as the doors slid closed.

"Damn it."

I watched the elevator light go up. Second floor. Third. And going. At least he was staying in the hotel. I scrambled to the stairway and up to the fourth floor, opening the door just enough to check the elevator. A couple of people were waiting for a car but all the doors were closed.

I returned to the steps and checked the fifth floor. Nobody. By the sixth, I was out of breath. When I pushed into the hallway, the elevator Connor had gotten in had just closed. I looked up and down the hall but didn't see him.

I ran toward an intersection in the hall and immediately ducked back. Connor was making his way down to the back of the building. I'd found him.

I took a deep breath and slipped out of the oversized jacket and pants. I didn't need the cover anymore and couldn't afford to be weighed down. Despite being down to the tank top, things were still claustrophobic.

Something was weird here. This was an older, less renovated part of the hotel. My brain was tight, like it was being squeezed. Strange things had been happening ever since I found the Horn of Subjugation. Things I didn't like. I shook it off.

After another second I peeked. Connor moved at a leisurely pace, only about halfway down the long hallway now. Instead of chancing exposure, I waited for him to choose a door.

The ding of the elevator announced another arrival.

Sergeant Ronaldo Garcia stepped out with another officer in BDUs.

"Hands up!" he shouted.

I didn't have time for this.

I drew a tentacle of shadow from the wall and wrapped it around the approaching officer in tactical gear. The wrap squeezed his gun to his body so he couldn't fire. Then I slammed him into the wall and he dropped to the floor.

Garcia didn't hesitate. His pistol barked at me. Blue energy sprouted from the tattoo on my palm. I had to force the Intrinsics to obey me more than usual—the black mark covering my hand was interfering with the tattoo—but the sergeant wasn't packing special bullets.

Lead bounced away in sparks as Garcia emptied his magazine. I charged. The sergeant backed away, but I caught him just as he finished reloading. I swiped the gun from his hand and butted it into the side of his head. KO-ed him in one hit. I dropped the gun beside him in irritation. After that gunfire, I'd just lost the element of surprise.

I hauled ass around the corner just in time to see the last door on the left closing. That was Connor. I had him, but we wouldn't be alone for long. I pushed myself down the hall, shutting out the claustrophobic presence. I passed a shadow, swiped my sawed off from the depths, and held it ready as I kicked open the door to the hotel room.

Empty. The fucking room was empty.

That couldn't be right. I'd seen him come in here. Damn the DROP team. Getting the DROP on Cisco Suarez. That joke gets old fast.

Connor was gone, but something remained. A faint charge in the air.

My green eyes filled with black, and I scanned the room for signs of spellcraft. The place was clean, but I could detect evidence of spirits. Not here, exactly, but close. Were they what clawed at my brain?

I withdrew my mirror and searched the room in its reflection, knowing there wasn't enough light to use it as a weapon. Useless. The mirror reflected the same things I saw without it. The bed. The window. The painting.

Wait a minute.

There was a painting hanging above the bed in the mirror, but it wasn't there when I looked straight at it. I furrowed my brow, wondering why I couldn't detect the abnormality with my shadow sight.

I took cautious steps forward, red alligator boots scuffing carpet, until I kicked open a hole in the world with a tear that sounded like paper.

This wasn't a hole in the world.

I put the mirror away and used my hands to rip the air ahead of me. A huge sheet of paper spanned the room from wall to wall, dividing it in half. But I didn't see the paper. I saw a facsimile of what was behind it, what I was supposed to see: an empty room.

When I ripped the enchanted paper, it fell away and the illusion flickered out. There I saw the painting that was really there, the one the illusion had failed to account for. But it wasn't the only anomaly.

There was an open door leading to the adjoining room

where Connor had fled to.

And there was Kita Mariko, the paper mage, standing between us, covering the man's exit.

Chapter 23

Kita slammed the door closed and we glared at each other. She was in a defensive stance, ready for my attack.

I ignored the paper mage and made for the door. She thrust her arm in the air and a flood of papers spilled from her sleeve like a deck of playing cards. The scraps each took on a life of their own and swerved toward me in a flock.

I shifted into the lowlight shadow and the attack whiffed through me. The projectiles spattered against the door Connor had escaped through. The papers crumpled and filled the gaps between the door and the frame, creating a quick-and-dirty seal.

I solidified and put a solid boot to the handle, but the door didn't budge. Connor was running, and Kita was helping him. I could deal with her, but he was aware of the threat now. I needed to find him fast.

I spun to the door I'd entered by. It had already closed itself, and before I could reach the handle, Kita waved her other arm, launching another assault from her sleeve. This time, I didn't bother entering the shadow. I sidestepped the swarm and watched it seal the last exit.

The paper mage smiled. "I can't let you at him," she said sternly.

"I'm not asking permission."

She narrowed her eyes and remained silent.

I raised the shotgun to her. "Open it."

"I can't," she said.

It wasn't beyond belief. Simple acts can have lasting consequences, not always easily undone. A lot of things in life work that way. I tried the handle, but it was stuck.

Kita didn't stay still. She reached into the fold of her jacket and threw down a folded paper, origami in the shape of a dog. It flashed yellow and grew in size, taking on animal form. Only this was no mutt. Her spellcraft had conjured an illusory four-legged dragon the size of a Great Dane. It growled at me, and I knew the regular birdshot I had loaded wouldn't slow it down.

I pulled the trigger.

The discharge was loud in the enclosed space. The pellets hit the wooden door in a small spread, punching a hole a few inches wide but otherwise leaving it intact. Kita snickered.

"I don't know what you're smiling about," I said. Then I phased into the shadow, becoming massless, shooting right through the small opening and solidifying on the other side of the door.

"Well, sh—" said Kita before I darted away from the sealed door.

The door to the adjoining room snapped shut. Connor raced down the hall. I left Kita behind, trapped by her own spellcraft.

At the end of the hall, instead of turning toward the elevators, Connor went the opposite way. The drug lord was making a run for something.

I followed around the corner, bending my shotgun in half and reaching for one of my special loads. Fireshot. I had a feeling Connor was more than human, and the voodoo fire had been effective against supernatural baddies before.

Ahead, Connor banged open a door to the access hall. A snapping sound followed. When I followed him in, I saw another door half open. This one heavier. It had been locked with a heavy chain. Now both ends dangled to the floor, their metal links molten orange.

I pushed the door in with my sawed off. Steps led up and down in darkness. A separate stairwell.

Except Connor was going up, away from the exit.

I followed the echo of his steps. We were in the iconic tower of the famous hotel, styled after the Tower of Seville. But I saw it in a different light.

The architecture was old. Narrow stairway, steep steps, with the stink of neglect. Deeper in the shadows, in a place only I could feel, I realized where the scratching at my brain was coming from.

The sensation wasn't pleasant, like the pressure a deep-sea diver feels. The darkness in the tower smothered my skin. There was resistance in the air here, and the higher I climbed, the thicker it got.

I phased forward through the shadow. Once. Twice. Rinse. Repeat. Any little gain to close the distance between us. I caught sight of the back of Connor's jacket as he rounded the next flight. I slid in the darkness, up and around, and materialized, holding my sawed off ready.

The top of the tower. A cramped, open-air platform with four archways in four walls. Nowhere left to run. Nowhere to hide.

Except Connor Hatch was gone.

No gates or glass prevented access outside. Once you moved through a window arch, your only option was a thirty-foot drop. I leaned out each cardinal direction, searching the roof and ground beneath, but there was no sign of Connor.

"How does he do that?" I muttered.

My eye ticked. A slight pain pressed the back of my head. It was foul up here. Whispering and scratching. I could practically hear the telepathic cries of the spirits. And they were coming on stronger.

I released my shotgun back to the shadow and found a piece of red chalk in my pouch. I traced a pentacle on the ground. A star, five points. Then I lit a birthday candle, dropped hot wax onto the middle of my mirror and glued the candle to it, and set it in the middle of the star. The voodoo knife came out next, but I hesitated. I'd cut myself with it countless times. This was different.

You don't pick up a five-hundred-year-old necromantic artifact and not learn a few things. I've mentioned that my senses have changed since finding the Horn, but really my abilities had always been changing. The Horn found me for a reason.

Even though I'd been hesitant to assume the power of the Horn, I had an ally in the Spaniard. He was a powerful necromancer in his own right (and likely an evil scourge to boot). But we were bound by a pact now, and the partnership came with perks. The wraith had taught me a trick or two.

This one creeped me the fuck out.

I sliced open the tip of my middle finger and squeezed till it suspended a healthy drop of blood. I brought that drop over the candle. The flame roared as my blood sizzled. My finger burned but I squeezed it more, coloring the mirror with blood. When the fifth drop landed on the glass surface, the entire room went crimson in a shockwave.

I wasn't alone. In fact, it was kind of cramped up here.

As kids, we used to point from the street, blocks away, and tell stories about this place. It was haunted. A World War II hospital that handled victims from the front lines. A dark and horrifying place, where depressed soldiers climbed the steps of this grand tower and welcomed oblivion with a jump.

I was surrounded by men—some missing limbs, some with disfigured faces. There was even a nurse, a ratchety woman with a bun so tight it pulled her face taut. I stared at the faces, trying not to show fear, not fully understanding how these ghosts stood before me.

Was this what the wraith meant by having one foot in the Murk?

"The red-haired man," I said. "Where is he?"

Below me, heels clacked against concrete steps.

"Where is he?" I demanded, leaving no room for insubordination.

The nurse raised her arm, her bony finger pointing out the north window. A blind man followed suit, but he signaled south. A soldier missing his nose, and another covered with burns, pointed east, and others west. One by one, each of the ghosts answered my query. If they were to be believed, Connor didn't go in *one* direction, he went in *all* of them.

"How's that possible?"

The racket from the stairwell echoed louder. The hard stares of the ghosts shifted. Kita Mariko turned the corner of the last platform before the top. The serpentine dragon made of paper was at her feet.

The attack dog charged up the steps. No longer armed with regular birdshot, I scooped up my shotgun and blasted it. A cone of fire disintegrated its face and shredded its body. The magical flames jumped along the paper surfaces. Even as the creature tried to split itself apart and save pieces, it was consumed by the fire. Within seconds, nothing but ash and smoke remained, drifting to the floor.

Kita's sharp eyebrows slanted into icy death. Still a flight below me, she reached to the small of her back and withdrew a bamboo stick, which she snapped open into a ruffled paper fan.

Shit. I'd faced her weapon before and it was sharper than anything I'd ever seen. It had even cut through my armored

Nordic tattoo.

"What is he?" I asked. "Where'd he go?"

Kita chuckled. She drew several paper balls from her jacket and tossed them on the ground. I flinched, but they just tumbled like dice. Then, slowly, each inflated with air, grew a few inches wide, and began to glow.

They were paper lights, getting brighter and brighter by the second. They twitched and hopped into the air, drifting on an invisible current and filling the tower with a brilliant light.

I blinked my shadow sight away before it blinded me. The ghosts and the redness of the room faded. Kita had probably never seen that anyway. But that wasn't her purpose. She was eliminating the ambient shadow, limiting my tool set, and making sure I couldn't shift behind her.

No place left to run.

Chapter 24

Kita smiled as her paper lights hovered around us. "You like them? I picked up a new trick after meeting you."

They definitely complicated matters. "I wanna know where Connor is."

"Beyond your reach," she taunted. "He'll be out of the country soon. You're one step behind him. Again."

"Off to his private island then?" She snapped her head up in surprise. She hadn't known that I knew. So it was true about the island. "Where is it?" I demanded.

Her face relaxed again. "The boss is gone, Cisco."

"I thought Rudi was your boss," I said sarcastically. Then it dawned on me. "You're not talking about the Society, are you?" My face darkened. "Connor's the head of the Covey. He's the one behind everything."

She shrugged. "You didn't already know? Emily, Tyson —we all get our marching orders from him. Even that cocky vampire who thought he could control you. I thought that's how you found us at his hotel."

Connor Hatch. He was the one who wanted the Horn and set the Covey on me. The gang war in Little Haiti, the real estate, the killing—he was the one responsible.

"Why are you working for him?" I asked.

"I like to back a winner."

"He didn't look like much running away." I cracked the shotgun in half and held it by the barrel in my left hand, like I just wanted to talk. I turned my body to the side so my belt pouch was behind me and casually reached in.

"He's a busy man. Don't think you're meaningful to him."

"I was meaningful enough to be murdered."

The paper mage scoffed. "That was Tunji's idea. To bring you into the fold and make you a powerful asset."

"Don't give me that. Connor had his eyes on me before that. The play from the start was to use me, a shadow charmer, to find the Horn of Subjugation. He set Emily against me to do that. What did he do, threaten her?"

Kita Mariko laughed. "Your sweet Emily, the damsel in distress? Cisco, whatever makes you think she didn't want to use you like that?"

I gritted my teeth. "I don't believe that."

She shrugged it off. "She made mistakes, Tunji made mistakes, even I underestimated you. We rarely agree on everything, but it works out in the end."

"The Covey's just one big dysfunctional family, is that it?"

"Something like that. We each have autonomy to do as we wish as long as it furthers his interests."

"The drug empire, you mean. The Passport to Latin America." I fingered the new shell I'd recently cooked up. "Connor's making inroads in Miami."

"Miami's only the starting point. We're moving into the whole country soon enough. Thanks in no small part to you." She was smug as she explained it, proud of what ten years of misery could accomplish.

"Killing your father. Setting me up. Starting a gang war. You did it all for a scumbag drug lord."

Kita fanned air to her face coyly.

"How did Connor disappear like that?" I demanded.

"You still don't know who he is." She said it matter-of-factly.

I spat on the floor. "He's a piece of garbage living on borrowed time."

"He's a jinn."

I froze. A jinn. A being from the Aether. A primal force, like an elemental, but independent, motivated.

The Aether is a place of fire and air. That explained how Connor could dematerialize out the tower windows and essentially vanish. Jinns are mysterious beings, not easy to face, usually only interacted with through intense protection measures and ritual binding.

I didn't try to hide the shock on my face, and it pleased Kita to see it. She grinned and took a step up while I worked the ramifications through my head.

The Earthly Steppe lies between the Aether and Nether. Being a connector realm, we're somewhat compatible with both, a sort of neutral ground. But the two extremes are polar opposites. Silvans and jinns do *not* get along.

That explained why Jade, in the hot tub, had cowered at the sight of Connor. If she somehow realized who he was, *what* he was, she would've been terrified.

That also partly explained his previous head of security, the Covey member still at large. Elementals aren't as ambitious as humans. They don't have the same agency, plotting, and scheming in our affairs. But jinns, not only are they familiar with subterfuge and manipulation, they're masters of them.

Worse, jinns are nigh untouchable.

I tried to discreetly slide the shotgun shell into the open barrel, but Kita finally caught on to what I was doing. She charged and raised the fan, but surprised me with a kick. Her high heel flew off as she batted my shotgun to the side. I managed to hold onto it, but the round bounced to the floor.

The hovering paper lights surrounded me next, and that's when the fan came down. Without a shadow to hide in, I threw up my forearm and braced myself. A wild flash of yellow met my armor as it flared blue. The powerful Intrinsics exploded and knocked us away from each other. I winced as my blood splattered to the floor where she had cut the tattoo. I didn't have a lot of those left in me.

Focused on her, I barely noticed the floating light dive at my side. I raised my energy shield just in time, snowflake tattoo searing through my black palm and manifesting a semi-sphere of blue energy, but it was no good. The shield was meant to stop velocity, items with very little mass. The paper light veered off course slightly but it passed through my defenses and crashed into my head.

A bright flash exploded within my eyeballs. Something within me faltered. My pull at what little shadow was left in the room weakened. It was like the light itself was consuming me.

I screamed. Kita swiped again and I rolled away, this time opting not to meet the sharp edge. I could only take so much of a beating at once, and I knew better than to underestimate Kita.

She came at me on my left while I was still disoriented. I hopped away and she spun around in a reversal. I was off balance and barely avoided getting my arm chopped off. But the fan sliced at my right hip, and I felt my belt pouch cut away. As I rolled backward, Kita kicked my spell tokens down the flight of stairs.

There went my ammo.

I waved my empty shotgun in the air, fending off the other balls of light. For the first time I wished the barrel hadn't been sawed off. The extra reach would've been useful now. But the remaining orbs didn't attack, and I figured Kita needed enough of them to stick around to provide light.

I scrambled away from the mage and searched for a better weapon, and then I realized we'd been standing in the midst of one the entire time.

I feinted and drew an attack from Kita before lunging toward the pentacle. As I skidded on the stone, my hand scraped the chalk away. Then I grabbed the mirror and slid it along the floor to Kita.

The pentacle was broken.

The air suddenly went cold and Kita paused her attack. A low rumble filled our eardrums.

"It doesn't matter how much light you have," I said to Kita. "There's enough darkness in this world to go around."

Then the birthday candle at her feet snuffed out. The remaining orbs of light went black and crumpled to the floor. Everything went dark.

That's when the scathing laughter erupted from the walls.

"What did you do?" she asked, spooked.

Soldiers materialized and reached for us. Kita swiped at them, but the ethereal beings ignored her attack. She screamed as claws tore at her flesh. In defense, a swarm of confetti and streamers filled the air around her, swirling in a tornado, attempting to shield her from the angry spirits.

I slid into the shadow, but even I wasn't immune here. Fingers tugged at me, scraping my soul. I exited the shadow on the other side of Kita and then my flesh was under attack too. I gritted my teeth and reached for the dropped shotgun shell. I rolled to my back, jammed it into the open barrel of the sawed off, and aimed at the flailing paper mage.

"You're not the only one who came prepared, Kita."

Then I blasted her with a new concoction, pebbles of ground bones and joints: the rendered basis of glue.

The particles smothered Kita with a substance that liquefied and thickened. It absorbed the paper tornado around her, soaked it till it was lifeless and saturated, and slapped it tightly against her body. In moments, her own defenses tightened around her like papier-mâché, pinning her arms and legs in place.

Kita screamed as the ghosts had free access to her. She tripped. Before she hit the ground, I tackled her. Together we barreled down the stairway, away from the prying hands of dead things. I scooped up my belt pouch and rolled her down another flight until we were safe. The hollow screams howled above before sputtering out as the spirits returned to their restless vigil.

The paper mage struggled on the floor like a flopping fish. I rolled her to her stomach and straddled her. Then I held my ceremonial knife to her neck and said, "Hold still."

She settled down and I cut away some of the gummy substance from her back. Her black satchel had been hung around her back the entire time. She'd kicked my ass wearing that and one high heel, but she was mine now.

"It's a dying art," I said, cutting her bag open and sliding out the laptop. "Paper. Everything's digital now." I found her phone in the bag as well and snatched it. "It's all over, Kita. Everything you worked for. I'm exposing it all."

She grumbled as I took her possessions, and I knew I didn't need the USB drive anymore. I leaned down to Kita and whispered in her ear.

"I made a promise that I wouldn't hurt you. You're practically family. But I want you to bow out of this."

Her eyes sharpened.

I held the blade closer. "I can't keep my claws back forever."

Her eyes set on the ceremonial bronze for a moment and then she nodded.

"Good," I said.

I left her there and slipped down the steps, using the darkness to cover my escape.

Chapter 25

My old truck sped down *Calle Ocho*. The late evening was darker in the Everglades, devoid of the frequent streetlights of the city. When I pulled onto the dirt road leading to my hideaway, I smiled. What self-respecting shadow charmer would have it any other way?

I'd last been here days ago, rushed out by the DROP team. Now, I didn't know what to expect. I entered the eyes of the tree frogs and the gators, flipping through them like security camera feeds. None reported anything more unusual than myself.

I parked and went to the glove compartment for another burner phone, but slammed it in frustration. I'd used them all and needed another batch. My funds were getting low but I could afford it. Sure, I didn't have an income, but it wasn't like I had expenses either. That's the great thing about abandoned boathouses in the wetlands. They're rent free.

I slipped inside with Kita's laptop. Everything was as I'd

left it. The fast food wrappers, the bedroll, even the five-hundred-year-old wraith standing beside the locked lead safe.

"You return, *brujo*. I feared you were dead."

"Too busy for that," I said. I set the computer down and flipped it open. It greeted me with a desktop image of the ocean. I shivered. I was good without the sea for a while.

I'm not the most technically savvy person, but the operating system was pretty much what I remembered, just with more rounded edges. Unfortunately, none of the files were named "Secret Drug Dealer Files" so I began the arduous task of searching the hard drive one folder at a time. All I'd wanted was to avenge my family. Instead, I had to play dirty Miami politics and chase money. Exposing Rudi was only the start.

The ghostly conquistador hovered a safe distance from me, both enraptured by and uncertain of the device. After nothing impressive happened, he spoke. "The police have not returned since their raid."

I nodded. "The silvans were true to their word then."

The skull smiled. "There is always a catch with the wild folk. They're twisted creatures. Abominations who exist to torment our kind. They get their hooks in and tug you with invisible lines, seeing you as utility and nothing else."

I shrugged. Ceela *had* used me to slow down Orpheus, but she'd delivered a powerful favor in return. "They're the least of our worries," I explained. "Rudi and Co. are connected. I uncovered quite a bit during my visit to the Cayman Islands."

The wraith cocked his head. "The Greater Antilles Archipelago."

"Whatever. Turns out there's a group of mages in a business alliance. Pretty much a cartel. Have you heard of the Society?"

The apparition only needed a moment before answering, "No."

"I've been getting their attention lately with some of my wilder stunts. They sent an enforcer after me. This guy was a lightning animist. A skeezy, two-faced, snake-oil-salesman sort. Said he wants a truce as long as I back down, but I'm sure he'd turn on me the second I was a liability."

"One occultist can be handled. He claimed an association with many?"

"That's the idea. But I have no way of knowing how big they are or how far their reach is. From what I've seen, I'm willing to bet they go deeper than a silvan's rabbit hole. But I haven't seen them stateside yet. Besides, the Society's not who I want." I looked up from the computer screen. "I found him. The head of the Covey."

"Excellent. Is he dead?" You gotta love the Spaniard.

"Not quite. I tracked him down to a fund-raiser. He's a drug lord building ties in Miami through Rudi Alvarez, strong-arming, and spellcraft. But he vanished into thin air before I could get to him. He's a jinn."

The wraith's red eyes flared brightly at the word. "Jinn." He tried it on his lips like a foreign delicacy, taking time to savor the fullness of it.

"You know something about them?"

"Jinns are worse than silvans."

"Anything else?"

The wraith shook his head. "A paltry amount."

"You told me you were well connected in life. That you had access to countless ancient texts, much of them now destroyed. Surely some of those books mentioned the jinn."

"Only stories."

"Can those stories help me stop him?"

The wraith sighed. It was a hollow sound that whistled through his bones. "I do not know if you can face a jinn. What I know is legend, and little more. It is said that there are three kinds of sapient beings in the world: man, jinn, and seraph. Seraphs are angels, a powerful but small race that guided us in our formative years. Less known to Westerners are the jinn, sometimes referred to as djinn or genies. Their kind is prevalent in ancient history—it is said King Solomon built his castle with jinn slaves—but that was a long time ago. Now seraphs are long gone but remembered, and jinns are still lurking but forgotten."

"That's mostly a fairy tale, though. There are lots of other races. Many that used to be human, but plenty foreign to the three."

"As I said, legends. But there is often truth to be found in sacred beliefs. Jinns are purported to be more like us than we know. They were given free will. They govern themselves, rule their own kingdom."

"The Aether."

The ghost nodded. "Other beings hail from the Aether, but the jinn are the dominant race there just as humans are on Earth and silvans below. All machinations of government go through them."

"So Connor comes down with an elemental buddy to wreak havoc on our steppe?"

"For profit," said the wraith. "But the elemental is unlikely a willing participant." The wraith turned to the safe that contained the powder horn he was bound to. "You know the tales, *brujo*. The genie in the lamp serving up wishes."

I nodded and played with Kita's phone while I listened.

"It is believed," he said, "the only safe way to handle a jinn is after it has been slipped into the noose of enchantment. Unable to channel its full power. I've seen it written that this particular trick of binding is rooted in jinn magic. A secret of their own kind, twisted and used against them to force them into servitude."

"And you think the elemental is in such a bind?"

"It would make sense, unless there's an elemental plot we're unaware of."

"Okay." I clapped my hands together. "Easy peasy. We can just cook up a binding spell then?"

"These arcane mysteries are beyond my knowledge, *brujo*. As you know, I focused my studies on the Murk and the spirits that give *us* power."

I frowned. Of course it wasn't easy peasy. "Jinns aren't powered the same way as us?"

"Humans tap spirits for magic. The wild folk are beings created from magic. It hums in their bones. The jinn, on the other hand, *are* magic. It is their essence, like all primal beings. That doesn't make them all powerful, but it makes them quite resilient. Foreign to our kind."

"But I'm smarter than the average bear," I quipped. "I should be able to slap him around a little. He ran from me back at the hotel."

The wraith blinked patiently. "Unless bound, escape is a jinn's safest bet. Exposed to open air, they can become one with the Aether instantly. Why fight when it is unnecessary?"

"I mean, this guy has a private jet. I've seen him hop into a car to avoid me. Why go through all that trouble?"

He thought a minute. "Jinns are unable to take objects from our physical world into the Aether. That's part of why binding them to a lamp is effective. Unless trusting others to the delivery, some business is best handled personally."

Money. Drugs. There were tons of reasons Connor might choose to use Earthly means of transportation. In the Caymans, he was carrying the USB drive. Back at the Biltmore, he just didn't have anything holding him down.

"Well, I'll be," I said, glancing at the map app on Kita's phone. An error message complained about not being able to update my location, but a map still loaded up. It was an old GPS coordinate from one of Kita's previous stops. And it was right in the middle of the ocean.

If I drew a line through the three Cayman Islands to Cuba, it intersected the location. It could've been a plane coordinate, I supposed. But maybe it was more. That line connected to the Sierra Maestra mountain range in Cuba. It was high ground that continued undersea and, in some areas, rose above the surface.

I'd found the location of Connor's private island.

"What is it?" asked the wraith.

I held out the phone to him. "Even Pablo Escobar can be cornered."

The Spaniard shied away from the phone. "Where did you get that?"

"Relax. It's called technology. You must've seen some by now."

"Not that," said the wraith. He lifted a finger of brown, shriveled flesh. "Your hand."

The hand holding the phone was completely covered in a dark crust. It was getting worse. I shrugged. "I mixed it up with a faun."

"That is not something to take lightly, *brujo*. You are cursed."

"So he said. But I haven't imploded or anything yet."

The Spaniard shook his head. "A Nether curse is less a magical hex and more a contract on your life."

Everything snapped into place. "That explains the mermaid."

"It is a stain that can only be given and taken by silvan royalty."

"Orpheus did say something about the Circle of Bone."

"That is his dominion then. You must convince them to remove it."

I snorted. "Not likely. You should've seen this guy."

The Spaniard's voice deepened. "As long as you bear that mark, the Nether will chase you. Scourgelings will be angered by your presence. Silvans will look to gain favor with their betters."

I nodded. "I kinda figured I should avoid the underworld for a while."

"They will grow bolder. They will come to the Earthly Steppe if they must."

I put the phone away. "I hear you but what can I do?"

"Beg for your life, or come to terms with the faun."

I answered him with a snicker. "That's not gonna happen. That guy's an asshole." At first I was surprised by the wraith's concern, but I realized if I died, so too did his chances for escape. He'd be bound to an artifact locked in a safe in the middle of nowhere for who knew how many more years.

"What about the others?" he suggested. "The satyr and the minotaur. Can they bargain on your behalf?"

I scratched my chin. If this Nether mark was as bad as the Spaniard insisted then Ceela still owed me. She seemed sensible, for a silvan anyway. "Maybe," I finally said. "I doubt it, but maybe. Only they're in hiding."

"I know where they are," revealed my companion. "When they entered the building, I hid from them. They never noticed me or your possessions, as you bid. After the human police were sent away, I overheard their plans."

Interesting. So I had a trick on the tricksters. But it had been days. There was no guarantee the silvans would still be there. I grimaced at the black crust spreading over my wrist. It was worth a shot, damn it.

But first, a quick stop.

Chapter 26

A cool breeze washed over the path outside Evan's house. I brushed the chill off my arms. The temperature had plummeted to the sixties sometime around midnight. Hey, that's pretty cold for Miami, and I didn't own a jacket.

A yellow Corvette pulled into the driveway and parked outside the garage. Evan Cross stepped out and ruffled his short, blond hair.

"Hey buddy," I said as I turned the corner of his house.

He started. "What the fuck? Everybody's looking for you." A pause. "*I'm* looking for you."

"Bang-up job then."

His demeanor remained harsh. "I'm in the shit because of you."

"Let me guess. Sergeant Ronaldo Garcia?"

"Not just him. Commissioner Alvarez. He's one of my bosses and he's holding me accountable."

I slid closer to my friend but kept my back against the

wall, staying in the shadow. "I'm not the trouble."

"Trouble," he scoffed. "You wanna hear about trouble, man?" He ticked out his fingers. "You kick-started a war in Little Haiti that included the death of a prominent Nigerian business leader. You broke into City Hall and attacked the chief of security. You trespassed onto the commissioner's private residence and assaulted him and his staff. Then you crash a private fund-raiser and attack my team. All using black magic."

"All magic's black when you don't understand it."

His face grew cold. "One of my squad officers died."

"That was the poltergeist. More fallout from the Covey. I'm sorry, Evan. I know Rudi's just a pawn. But he's chosen sides so I'm taking him down."

He laughed. "You can't take him down, Cisco."

I held out the laptop. "With what's on here, I sure can. Now I'm hoping *you* choose a side, buddy, and I hope it's the right one."

"I'm a cop. Of course I'm on the right side."

"Then take the laptop."

We stood in silence for a minute, sizing each other up. He was probably working out how to get me into cuffs so he could turn me in. I was taking a gamble on my friend, but it was a good bet as far as I was concerned.

He eyed my offering warily before taking it from my hands. "What's on here?"

"Account records from Blue Sky Investments in Grand Cayman. A shell for the real estate being plucked and sold along Biscayne Bay. But that's just the start of it. The war in

Little Haiti, devaluing those properties, me being a hit man thrall for the Covey—it's all just a small piece. On this hard drive are bank accounts and fraudulent activities that directly tie to Rudi Alvarez. Shit, Kita kept so much dirt on him, I wouldn't be surprised if she was blackmailing him herself."

He nodded but was already thinking about something else. "Kita recorded these? Where is she?"

I hiked my shoulders. "I thought she was at the hotel."

"She disappeared during the Biltmore incident. I asked you not to hurt her, Cisco."

"I only roughed her up a little. Listen, her disappearing is good news. I asked her to get out of all this. She's probably on the run." When he didn't say anything, I added, "She's fine. Trust me."

"You're making that harder and harder," he said. "But okay. I'll take a look at these files."

I smiled, happy to see my faith being upheld. "I, uh, didn't see your name in those investments, by the way."

He looked away. "The accounts were never in my name. They were in Emily's. But we cleared out of the deal after you told us the money was dirty. Stupid as it was, we left a lot of cash on the table."

I grinned wider. "You can still be on the right side of this, then."

"I already am. Any illegal activity was done without my knowledge, Cisco. Believe me."

I nodded. "I do."

"Thanks, uh, for trusting me too."

"Hey, you gotta trust someone." I scratched the back of my head. "So listen. If this all works out..."

"You wanna see Fran."

"Pretty much." I didn't care about telling her I was her father. Not yet, anyway. The last thing I wanted was to turn her world upside down. But I wanted to be part of it.

"Maybe," Evan said. "But that's a long maybe. I can't have my child interacting with a known fugitive."

"I get it. Once I get Rudi off my back, I'll be anonymous in Miami again. It'll be safe."

He frowned and I knew what he was thinking. Things would never be safe around me. I didn't buy that. Once the Covey was out of the way, everything would change for the better. We stood there in silence until it started to get awkward.

"There's just one more thing," I said meekly. "In the spirit of open communication and all. I've known for a couple weeks, but I didn't know how to tell you. Maybe I was afraid of what I might learn. It's... it's about Emily."

Even with the laptop, he managed to cross his hands over his chest and look superior.

"She's a member of the Covey."

He blinked at me. "This group you're chasing?"

I nodded.

He swallowed hard. "What are you saying?"

I hissed. Did he ever listen? "The people that had me killed, Evan. She and Kita were a part of that. Their father too."

His eyes turned angry. "Bite your tongue."

"It's true. I already confronted her about it. That night with the poltergeist. When you were stuck with the cleanup at Rudi's house, I visited her here."

My friends arms dropped slowly to his side. "You shouldn't be coming here without me around."

"Are you even hearing me, bro? Emily's involved."

Still stoic. "Screw that. I don't want you bothering her about this."

I dropped my head and closed my eyes. I knew this would hurt him. "She admitted it to me, Evan."

I heard a click as Evan pulled the hammer back on his Colt Diamondback. I opened my eyes slowly. My friend had pulled a gun on me.

"Quick draw," I whispered. Had he been waiting the whole time for an opening?

"You remember when you thought I'd betrayed you, Cisco? You remember when you had that slither of darkness around my neck? How angry you were? You could have killed me."

We both stood like statues. I could've made a move, but I didn't.

Evan lowered the gun. "This was the opposite time, *buddy*. Your life was in my hands. Remember that."

I nodded.

He holstered his weapon and stomped to the front door, but turned for one last word of warning.

"The shit that's happened to you—no one deserves that. But now you're talking about my family. *My* family. You leave them the fuck alone, or I won't be so nice next time."

I let him go inside with the sum total of evidence I had against Rudi Alvarez. I guess, in hindsight, that could've gone better.

Chapter 27

One of the islands south of Miami Beach is Virginia Key. Most people know it because of the Miami Seaquarium. That or they take the Rickenbacker Causeway over it to get to Key Biscayne. But there's plenty of land in Virginia Key. More to it than people know.

Miami Marine Stadium was built in the sixties to showcase motorboat racing on the Bay. A backdrop of the islands and the downtown skyline made for a stunning view. But in the early nineties, Hurricane Andrew swept through the city. Miami Marine Stadium was declared unfit and shuttered its doors for good.

Not that it really *has* doors. The stadium's an open-air slab of cement straddling the beach and the water. A row of pillars behind the seating holds an enormous concrete roof that slopes sharply overhead, leaving nothing for the audience to see but clear blue sky and water.

I turned off the pickup's lights before I rolled into the

empty parking lot. I'd never actually been here before. Just another piece of history lost to the generations. That didn't mean the stadium didn't show signs of life.

As I skirted the concrete access ramp that led to the seats, it was clear this place was never truly abandoned. Every square inch of the structure, including the metal hand railings, was covered in graffiti. Black, red, blue, green; I was surrounded by a rainbow of symbols and tags. On the way up, two Cuban kids not even old enough to smoke strolled by holding cans of spray paint. We nodded at each other and passed. Behind me, the clacker in their paint cans rattled as they readied for another piece of street art.

When I crested the ramp, I stood on a platform that horizontally divided the seating area in the center. The wooden chairs, cracked paint and all, rode right down to the waterline without even the safety of a railing. Only a thin cement walkway like the one I was on prevented a view from turning into a bath. In the first row were two more street artists, one a ropey black kid and the other a teenage girl. Puerto Rican, I thought. Both relaxed in the chairs, watching the water.

The Bay was calm today, a far cry from the choppy waves the night before. I turned to scan the rest of the seats but didn't see anyone else. A skyway above led to a floating press box. Despite having open windows, it was the only area in the stadium that could be described as enclosed. My money was on the silvans holing up in there.

I took a couple steps up the staircase before I stopped myself and turned around, a chuckle on my lips. Then I headed down the stairs instead, to the third row, and sat behind the couple watching the water.

"If I were on the run," I said smoothly, "the last thing I'd do is leave my back to the entrance." The two kids turned around, and the Puerto Rican girl's nose wiggled in that way I found so cute. I winked at her. "Just sayin'."

Ceela and Throok were in their human guises, but there were still plenty of similarities. Ceela's eyes were smaller, less exaggerated, but the same confident orbs sparkled within. Large gold hoops hung from each ear. Throok was imposing, even in his chair two rows below me, with a stripe of red across the center of his hair and through his matted beard. Their clothes were unassuming—jeans, baggy black shirts—and, of course, they had human legs. Silvans were masters of glamour, at least when it came to generalities, but they didn't possess magic to completely transform themselves. They couldn't change faces or skin color or height.

"At least you ditched the nose hoop," I told Throok.

He turned away from me and growled. Ceela clapped him on a big shoulder and laughed, taking it in stride.

"I'm impressed, wizard," she said, looking me over. "You've performed excellently."

A gruff snort. "I'm surprised you're still alive."

I ignored the crankypants. "You've done well for yourselves too, I see. Keeping your glamours on in our steppe for this long has to be taxing."

Ceela hiked a small shoulder. "Some might think so."

"You also did as you promised," I said. "My friend

reported that the police abandoned my hideaway quickly after your arrival, and they haven't been back."

Throok spun around. "There was no one else there, wizard."

I clucked my tongue. "If that's true, then how'd I find you?"

They traded a nervous glance. I admit, I was impressed at the wraith's ability to hide as well. Neither the police nor the silvans detected his presence. I supposed keeping a foot in the Murk had its benefits.

The satyr chuckled abruptly, a bit too forcefully, pretending to be unruffled. "One of your pet spies. Of course!"

I didn't correct her. Ceela played it off but she was flustered by their lack of discretion.

"We shouldn't be near him," warned the minotaur.

"Our deal was done," she said, dismissing the subject. "We have no more business, Cisco Suarez."

"That's not exactly true," I said, presenting my left hand to them. "There's a snag that's not tied up. The little detail of a Nether mark."

The two avoided looking at the black crust wrapping my skin.

Throok turned away from me again. "This is trouble, Ceela. We should go."

She was less dismissive. "What do you expect from us?"

"I expect *something* because this is your fault. You owe me."

She huffed and crossed her arms, like what I was asking

was impossible.

I leaned over the empty row of seats. "I heard silvan royalty can remove the black mark. Do you two have any connections?"

Their eyes locked. Then Throok snorted. "Not just any royalty, wizard. That is a faun curse. It must be lifted by faun royalty."

Great. Silvan society was full of arbitrary rules and addendums. It was a lot like American bureaucracy, or the US tax code. I wondered if they had lawyers whose entire job was interpreting the ancient ways.

"The Circle of Bone," explained Ceela. "I did grow up close to one. He was a friend that doted on me."

"Perfect," I said. "Let's talk to him."

She leveled her eyes flatly at me. "He's Orpheus."

I rolled my eyes. "The baron of the Circle of Bone."

"Barons," grunted the minotaur. "I—"

"Let me guess," I cut in. "You hate them."

Throok nodded. "Spoiled royalty, with their castes and proprieties."

The satyr pulled her head back. "Don't say that."

"You know what I mean," he said. "It's the reason we're in this situation."

I hopped a row of seats to get right behind them. "How so?"

They looked at each other and Ceela sighed. "Here it is. Orpheus is a powerful man. He stands to inherit quite a bit. But he's the youngest of three brothers, and the least qualified to take over the Bone. It's not going to happen.

You see, he can be a bit whiny when he doesn't get what he wants."

"And that's you?"

She nodded. "I don't know how, but he bartered for my hand in marriage. By all precepts, I should be his."

"And you don't get a say?"

"Not this time. He's asked nicely before and I've refused. Every time." She sighed. "He had tender moments in his youth, but I don't love him."

Throok snorted. "The sniveling coward went above her head."

"Given his height," I said, "that's a tall order." Nobody laughed.

"I do have recourse," continued Ceela. "There is no rule of law forcing my hand, you see. It is an agreement between families, less of an arrangement and more of a bet. Orpheus was given seven days to stake his claim. Ten hours from now, when the sun sits at its peak in your sky, I will be free."

"What happens then?" I asked.

"His claim expires."

I wrinkled my forehead. "Just like that, he'll stop trying?"

Throok chuckled. "I can be convincing."

Ceela smiled and shook her head. "My friend won't need to intervene. And Orpheus will not stop trying to gain my favor. But he will abide by the wager. It is the way of our people."

I shook my head. What did I tell you about silvan politics?

"So for the next ten hours, you want me to wait around

while every silvan kissing up to faun royalty tries to take me out?"

She smiled and wriggled her nose. Not so cute this time. "You've lived this long. I'm sure you can manage another night."

I frowned, wondering how much they were telling me was true. "How about I just stick around with you two until then? A sort of insurance."

Throok snorted loudly. His eyes turned red and a gold earring appeared, hanging on his nose. "You do not realize the danger you're putting us in, wizard. You must go or—"

"Danger?" I scoffed. "You're one to talk."

Ceela cut in. "He's right, Cisco Suarez. That stain you wear is a beacon to our kind. It marks you as quarry. Gives the hunters a target."

My words caught in my throat. I wondered again if I was being played, but their faces were dead serious. Call me a sucker, maybe. Cisco Suarez the sap. But don't call me cruel. Suddenly I understood why Romeo and Juliet were on edge.

A voice rang out from the platform above us. "You should listen to the kids," it said. "They know what they're talking about."

We all stood and faced the interloper (but not before Throok scowled at me like I was an idiot).

"Stay here," I muttered as I moved to the aisle and headed up the concrete stairs. I checked the rest of the stadium as I climbed, but as far as I could tell, he'd come alone. Alarms in my head still went off, though, no more overt than niggling static against my skin.

In the breezeway stood Simon Feigelstock with a salesman's smile.

Chapter 28

I met the man on the middle platform.

"How're you doing, Thunderer?"

He grinned and spread his hands. "Better than you, Dead Man." I didn't like the nickname. "What you've got here is a conundrum. Only it's not the conundrum you think."

"Leave them alone," I warned.

He chuckled and shook his head. "You see? That's what I'm talking about. You're missing the point entirely." The lightning animist cupped his hands around his mouth like a megaphone and yelled down to the silvans. "I'm not here for you," he said, all easygoing charm. "Whatever you two are into is your business. I only ask for the same courtesy. Cisco and I have our own dealings to attend to."

Ceela and Throok remained ready but didn't budge from the edge of the water. That was smart for a couple of kids. Simon turned to me and muttered under his breath. "Really, Cisco, is your life such a wreck that you're slumming with high schoolers now?"

"What are you doing here?" I asked with deadly focus.

The wizard let his smile drop. "I warned you not to intervene in political matters."

"I guess we forgot to shake on it."

"We still can." He extended his hand. A string of blue lightning arced between his thumb and index finger. "But I'm a squeezer."

I put my hand up to signal Ceela and Throok to stay away. Good job, Cisco. Like they were swarming in to defend me anyway. Whatever. It was better if they stayed out of this, tricksy silvans or not. None of us knew what Simon was capable of, but I could tell he was a pro. He already had tabs on me in Miami.

"How'd you find me?" I asked.

"I noticed that black hand in the Caymans. Any silvan with a pulse could've found you."

I turned to my friends downstairs. Well, acquaintances really. If they were the ones who'd sold me out, I might need to unfriend them on Facebook.

"Stay behind me," directed Throok, moving ahead of the satyr.

I took a step away from Simon. "You're not gonna fight me openly. Not with them here."

Simon grimaced and considered the otherwise empty stadium for a long moment. Then he turned to me with a devilish smirk. "They're not human, are they?"

Before I could answer, his hand came up and flashed white-hot blue. I slithered to the side in the shadow, but the javelin of lightning seared across my back anyway. I stumbled in pain, but I'd closed the distance between us.

I clocked Simon in the jaw, sending him stuttering. Frankly, I was surprised he was still on his feet. I followed with a blow to his stomach. He doubled over and I heaved him into the air, ready to suplex him against the metal railing.

Before I did, a world of pain surged through me. Simon's entire body coursed with electricity. It was all I could manage to break away from him.

"Fast," he said as we both rose to our feet. "But you can't outrun lightning."

"I don't want to hurt you," I said.

He scoffed.

I tried to come off less aggressively. "You're starting a war with the wrong person."

He raised his eyebrows expectantly. "You gonna lay off Commissioner Alvarez?"

"Not until he's disgraced and out of a job."

"Wrong answer," he said. He held his arms out and drew sparks of power from the open sky. Then he lashed out with both fists and a raw bolt of energy came at me.

In the full shadow of night, I usually felt pretty safe. This time the darkness could not cloak me. Simon's spellcraft created light. By its nature it dispelled my source of power, if only for fleeting moments. The bolt of magical lightning hit me like a bus square in the chest.

I tumbled down the concrete steps, bumping and rolling until the narrow platform at the bottom stopped my fall. Besides getting the Frankenstein treatment, I'd picked up a couple of knocks on the head. Just trying to focus made me dizzy.

I stood, drew my knife, and took a step up to him. I didn't even see the lightning that cracked into my hand. I slammed back to the floor again and lost my weapon somewhere.

Throok watched silently as I climbed to all fours.

"You know," said Simon, adjusting his cufflinks. "Everything I said about our organization was true. But still you chose to ignore the power of—what did you call me —'dime-a-dozen cartel muscle?' That really hurt."

As soon as the wizard took a single step down, I drew my shotty from the deep and let it bark. Simon jerked backward as a shower of red and blue sparks erupted from his gut. Birdshot flew everywhere, tearing holes in the wooden chairs around him.

"Whoa!" he said, his face brightening. "That was fast! What did I tell you?" He brushed the shirt between his open jacket but I hadn't even left a mark. The man had his defenses up. An invisible sheen of pure energy had deflected every single scattered projectile.

He turned to the silvans with amazement, eyes wide like he'd just seen an impressive touchdown throw. Then Simon smiled and focused on me. "My turn."

He threw another bolt at me. This time I met his open hand with mine, drawing power through the Norse tattoo on my palm, the Helm of Awe. Turquoise energy, this time my own, flared to life in a semi-sphere that I ducked behind. Simon's lightning crashed into my shield, and I bit down as my arm shuddered under the pressure.

This wasn't a simple projectile, like a bullet. But lightning was massless. My shield could counter the supernatural as well as the mundane as long as it was more energy than object. But physics and magic both required that energy be dispersed somewhere. The lightning flared away from me, jumping this way and that, but some of it made it through to my body.

Luckily, by this point, I was quite familiar with pain.

The wizard pulled back his magic and growled. "You're just a walking bag of tricks, aren't you?" He let out a furious scream that rose in pitch, and I saw it. The water leaned toward us like a glass tilted to the side. The air grew more crisp. He was drawing in more power, readying for a heavier blow. One that I might not be able to withstand.

I kicked my boots and rose. I only managed one step before I collapsed on the ground again. My body was still reeling. In shock. When the next bolt of lightning came, it was all I could do to get my shield up again.

This time the electricity came in a constant stream, thicker and more overpowering. I convulsed under the indirect power of the blast. Even with the shield, he was zapping me. My teeth scraped and my neck twisted to the point of breaking, but I knew, if I let down my guard, I would die.

Still blasting away, Simon forced himself closer, descending to my level. Each step nearer, the pressure on me intensified. My eyes turned to the silvans. Throok wore a grim mask, unhappy with what was happening but watching passively. Even with Ceela appealing to him from behind, he held her back, refusing to put her in danger.

And that's when I saw that he loved her.

Nothing, no matter how tragic or despicable, compares to losing a loved one. Fear pulls our heartstrings from all directions, forcing us to constantly compromise. Like Evan refusing to blame his wife. Like them keeping Fran from me. Safety is paramount, and the more people you let in, the more nerve-racking it can get.

After the horrors I'd caused my family, I wasn't sure I blamed the minotaur.

I winced as Simon stood over me, electricity flowing from his hand to mine. My body was numb, barely listening to my brain anymore, but somehow the signals got through. Simon's face twisted into an indignant snarl, and he reached down for me.

I uppercut my shadow fist into his chest.

The force propelled Simon away in a blinding flash. I had no idea what his defenses could do, but I was starting to get an idea. The enforcer shrugged off the attack like it was a playful shove. It displaced him, sure, but his electrical field had mitigated the shadow. And I'd put a lot into that punch.

I nearly passed out from the effort, again struggling to stand. My body didn't want to listen.

Simon carefully stepped down to me, his comb-over sticking up off his head in all directions. Noticeably absent was his smug smile.

I tried to push him off but lightning shocked me into submission. I drew away. He clamped his arms around my throat. Something scraped my neck and I fell on my back. Simon squeezed, spittle dripping from his lips in zeal.

His attack charged through me, sending my entire body into convulsions. I clenched my jaw and tried to push him off, but the onslaught was too much. I was amazed at Simon's command of the Intrinsics, the amount of raw power he was able to channel. It put anything I could manage to shame.

From the bloodlust apparent on his face, I knew the wizard wasn't gonna let up. Simon wasn't gonna just choke me, he was gonna electrocute me. I forced my muscles through the pain. I clawed for my knife but it was a step above us. Out of reach.

Then I felt something else. It wasn't pain—I had plenty of that to go around, believe me—but I sensed a different kind of spellcraft. Something I'd felt a long time ago. The lightning kept surging, but something else snaked through my neck and into my arteries. Whatever it was, I knew it was far more dangerous than the lightning.

I clawed weakly at Simon's face. All the hairs on my arm stood on end. I shook uncontrollably. I thought I had a lot of fight, but Simon was breaking something in me, something that made me who I was. Something I didn't want to lose. I thought my heart was about to stop. My arm dropped to the floor as the resistance left me completely. Simon smiled...

And promptly got kicked in the face.

Chapter 29

It was a blur. Simon flew off me. Something tall and large lumbered overhead. I reeled in the aftershock of pain. Clipped words were shouted, but I couldn't make them out. I gripped the floor to stop the world from spinning.

After what felt like agonizing minutes, the horizon steadied. My pupils cracked open and filled my irises, and I got my focus back, too.

Throok had engaged Simon. No longer wearing his glamour, the minotaur was all muscles, hooves, and fur, with menacing horns jutting from his head. Throok wielded his bent kukri.

Simon, despite being sucker punched, had managed to get enough of his defenses up to save his life. He was quick, too. Vital to a long life as an animist.

Throok was fresh, managing to keep the enforcer's spellcraft at bay with a series of quick strikes. It was a relentless assault. Each blow, however, was met with a crackle of light. And although Simon looked the worse for wear, I knew the minotaur would tire first.

Ceela watched nervously, no doubt told to stay put by her bodyguard.

I guess there's no rest for the wicked.

I dug for another of my custom shotgun shells, but my pouch was running low. Just two rounds left. Hey, you can't call me out on lack of preparation. Blame the spriggan army for my dearth of ammunition. I squeezed the final fire payload, snapped the sawed off closed, and then palmed a handful of gray powder.

Between Throok's strikes and Simon's feints, it would've normally been a tough brawl to tag into, but I had the night on my side. I charged them and slid through the shadow, popping in right beside them. With a forceful exhale, the powder puffed into the air and clouded around Simon.

His electrical field crackled, hissing and spitting like water in hot oil. I couldn't tell if anything was getting through, but Simon must've been waiting to see my play. He lowered his head and lurched forward, suddenly becoming an unstoppable train of electricity.

I raised the shotgun but he barreled into me first. My weapon clattered to the cement. It spun on its side like a top, barrel and handle scraping toward the edge of the platform. It stopped with the trigger balanced precariously over the water. Another inch and it would've been swallowed by the sea.

"Take him from both sides!" shouted Throok, already clambering over the seats and getting the high ground on the mage.

I approached from an equal level, on the bottom, gathering shadow into my hand. Lightning magic might dissolve that darkness on contact, but if I struck when Simon was distracted, it might be able to get through. If not, I'd just need to hit him again and again until his defenses wore out or my arm fell off.

We started to converge on Simon, but Throok panicked when he saw the animist backing away. Simon had reversed the battlefield, retreating closer to Ceela.

The minotaur swung a wild overhand strike at him before I could engage. The enforcer lifted his hand and lightning cracked out, consuming Throok's kukri. He roared and dropped the hot weapon, favoring his hand. The minotaur was in trouble.

I rushed forward, but Simon was good. He anticipated our moves and knew who to strike first to stay alive. As I came at him with a magically empowered haymaker, the lightning wizard smiled and reached out for me.

He would've caught me, too, if Ceela hadn't weaseled into his head.

She chanted and waved her hand. Simon wobbled, almost as if his muscles forgot to stand up for a second. But he righted himself. He was dazed but fighting off the satyr's sleep spell.

Simon was too strong for such hexes. Most animists were. But he hadn't expected it, and it slowed him just enough to distract him.

My shadow fist slammed into his jaw in a gout of brilliant sparks. His defenses were active, but unfocused. The darkness seeped through and twisted his head to the side, slinging blood into the air. The wizard careened across the ground before landing unceremoniously in a heap at Ceela's feet.

"No!" cried the minotaur.

I couldn't believe my eyes, but the scrawny, balding Simon Feigelstock shrugged off my blow and whipped around Ceela. He wrapped his arms around her waist and stunned her with electricity.

The surprise wore off quickly. Ceela forced a skinny elbow into Simon's stomach, but electricity battered her arm away. It must've hurt, but the satyr kept at it. Her lower half transformed into strapping horse legs and she planted a hoof into his knee. The blow should've forced the mage into six to eight weeks of bed rest. Instead, Simon ignored her, palmed something in his hand, and held it against Ceela's neck.

Throok and I froze.

I couldn't see if the enforcer held a knife or not. Whatever it was, it was small. The threat was enough for Ceela, though. She'd completely stopped resisting.

After a tense breather, Simon relaxed enough to unclench one hand and use it to fix his collar. Then he leaned over and spit out a loose tooth. The enforcer's eyebrows were up again. He chuckled nervously and said, "Whoa, man. That was intense."

Throok and I exchanged a troubled glance. Simon was an odd duck, both quirky and deadly. That combination made for an unpredictable adversary. The last advantage he needed was a hostage.

"I will kill her," he said coolly to the other silvan. "This wasn't your fight, but it is now."

"Let her go," pleaded Throok. "We'll walk away if that's what you want."

Gee, thanks.

Simon shook his head. "Too late for that. You kids wanted a fight, go at it then."

We looked at each other, confused.

"Do I need to spell it out?" asked Simon. "You have a choice, minotaur. You can attack me and risk your pretty little darling here, or you can take down Cisco and earn my favor." He scraped his fist against Ceela's neck. "Guess which one I think you should choose."

Throok and I eyed each other again. I chuckled at the ridiculous offer. The minotaur leaned down in the row of seats. His kukri scraped against the concrete as he picked it up and faced me.

"You're kidding," I said. "Really?"

"I have no other option, wizard. If I had let him kill you then Ceela would be safe. I took a chance and failed." He walked along his row to the aisle and then came down to meet me.

"But we're not going to actually fight," I asserted. "That's ridiculous. We should work together to save her."

Simon let electricity arc threateningly between his fingers. "How long do you think she could take a surge of my power?"

I wasn't sure. Satyrs weren't weak, but they were

certainly more brittle than minotaurs or zombie-skinned dead men. I couldn't consider the question any further because I had to turn my attention to the seven-foot-tall minotaur who stomped toward me with no intention of slowing down.

"Okay, what's the plan?" I whispered when he was near.

Throok swiped the kukri at my neck. I phased under his legs and materialized. He spun around and grunted. "I *hate* that trick."

He lashed at me again. This time I slid up to the third row, forcing him to vault a couple chairs. Before he knew it, I was at the bottom again, working my way closer to Simon.

"Oh, come on," complained the enforcer. "You've got to be kidding me. All brawn and no brains, aren't you?" He grumbled, upset at the stalemate.

The minotaur ripped a chair from the floor and threw it at me, attempting to anticipate where I would land, but I juked right and went left, leaving him two rows of chairs away once more. His chest heaved as his strikes wore him out, and still I got ever closer to Simon, pretending not to notice.

Only Simon's sour face brightened. "This is ridiculous. But I can see how much Little Miss Cloppity means to you, so I have a new plan." He reached into his pocket and threw a glass orb on the floor behind him. It shattered and an orange bubble grew in its place. "Rudi Alvarez is untouchable," he said. "I don't care what you discovered or what you have. If word gets out, if he takes a fall, then this arm candy gets the electric chair."

As he turned away, his eyes lingered on me. "And don't worry, Cisco. We won't forget about all this. I gotta hand it to you. You're stronger than even the Society thought."

I raised a tendril of shadow behind him. "Tell me something I don't know."

He exchanged a glance with Ceela, shrugged, and said, "There's a mermaid behind you." Then he jumped into the bubble.

I snatched the whip of shadow at him but his words slowed me. Two hands grabbed my ankles and yanked me off the concrete platform. I clawed at a pole, a vestige of an old railing no longer around. Sure enough, a mermaid pulled me to the water from behind. Her ruby tail splashed as she furiously tried to drag me under.

Gemma. A silvan. The Nether mark. That explained how Simon tracked me.

Gripping the edge of the platform, all I could do was watch helplessly as Simon's bubble closed around him and his hostage. The orange sphere blinked out by the time Throok swiped at him.

A shrill scream rang out as Gemma tugged harder. I lost my grip and my chin hit the floor, but I managed to hang on. Unfortunately, Throok was more concerned with Ceela's disappearance than my current predicament.

My boots kicked in the water now, trying to keep the mermaid off me. I knew that once I fell in, my shadow magic would be nullified. But here, on solid ground, I could still pull off a trick or two.

A new shadow tendril unfurled from the cement. My

shadows don't have the finesse to hold objects nicely, but in this case, a simple nudge would do. The darkness propelled my dangling sawed-off shotgun over the edge of that platform. It fell through the air and I caught it just before it hit the water. Then I turned it over my back to my attacker.

Gemma released me as I pulled the trigger. A cone of fire blasted from the short barrel and washed over the mermaid as she dove underwater.

I dragged myself over the edge of the platform and stared into the water, past the boiling bubbles and the dying fire rippling on the current. A flash of movement disappeared into the depths. A single red scale floated to the surface.

Heavy hooves clomped toward me. I spun around to see the minotaur towering above, scowling and brandishing his kukri.

Chapter 30

"Wizards!" bellowed Throok.

I skidded away on my back. "Whoa there, big guy."

Throok snorted. "I *hate* wizards."

"Anyone ever tell you you're single-minded?"

He growled. "This is clearly your fault."

"I admit, a little more open communication between us could've avoided some trouble, but we've both made mistakes here. Can you please stop lumbering now?"

"I'm not lumbering, I'm walking."

I tilted my head. "You should see yourself."

He hissed and sheathed his short sword. As he did, his form shifted back to a man. A boy, really.

"Relax," he said. "You had the right idea back there. I only attacked you as a show to distract the wizard."

"But you were really swinging that thing at me."

"Don't be a baby. I've seen you work your shadow magic."

I sighed in relief. I didn't feel like a baby.

I sat up and checked the water again. No dead mermaids floated to the surface. I scooped up the single red scale, translucent under the moonlight.

"You hit her," said the minotaur.

"She's still alive." I cursed. As long as I wore this black mark, she'd find me. Note to self: Beef up my gator guard back in the Everglades. I'd make her regret swimming into those swamps.

"Listen," I started, getting to my feet and collecting my things. "You need to broaden your horizons. Not all animists are bad news. That guy and his Society? I don't want anything to do with that business."

"On the contrary," he rumbled, "his issue is that you are irrevocably tied to his business."

The big dummy had a point. "You don't understand. The people he's protecting, they did things. They killed me."

Throok arched an eyebrow and looked me over. "Killed you?"

I shrugged and put on my best Monty Python accent. "I got better." He didn't get the reference. I shook my head. "What are we even talking about, anyway? The bottom line is, he took Ceela. And he used some kind of teleportation package to escape, so he could be anywhere."

The minotaur grunted as a young couple entered the stadium. We had an audience again, even if they were mostly concerned with sitting in the back row and locking lips. Throok stroked his red goatee.

"This is what troubles me," he said. "That man, that

wizard, he shouldn't have been able to take her."

I bit. "Why not?"

"She's too powerful to be manhandled by a human. I protect her from the worst of it, but her enchantments and glamours should've kept her safe."

"I don't know. That sleep incantation she tried was small potatoes."

He grunted. "It did what was intended. But I meant her defenses. That wizard shocked her into submission too easily. That should've been impossible. He wasn't even strong enough to beat you."

"Hey! What're you trying to say?"

"Stow your ego." He turned to the sea, contemplating the problem. "Ceela's no normal satyr. She's special among her kind. A principesse of the Juniper Circle."

A silvan princess. It all clicked into place. Orpheus, the baby of the family, seeking to improve his station and gain influence with other silvan circles. If Ceela was a true principesse, I could see why Throok wasn't supposed to mingle with her. And I could see why her future was being arranged.

I rubbed my neck as I thought of Simon squeezing the life out of me. I was starting to think Throok had a point about us missing something. There wasn't just lightning coursing through my body. There had been something else, something that stirred my soul. An odd bit of spellcraft that had left me dazed. It might've gotten me if Throok hadn't stepped in.

I then thought of the glass object he used to teleport

with.

"So he had help," I concluded. "And you're not gonna like who that is." Throok turned to me and waited expectantly, hands clenched, ready to mete out justice to whoever I named. "It's a jinn."

The minotaur jerked away from my words as if they could infect him. Silvans and jinns don't mix. And Connor couldn't be further from the minotaur. One was all cunning and discretion, the other muscle and action. Throok's face darkened. "I *hate* jinns."

"Big surprise. From what I understand, he can disappear whenever he likes. But he can't bring Ceela with him. And that teleportation package has to be a limited resource. So he'll have her stashed somewhere safe." I thought of all the various properties where Simon and Connor could hide. What didn't I know about? Where couldn't I find them? Then I had it.

"The private island," I said. "Ceela's being held in the sea between the Caymans and Cuba. A drug lord's haven. If we could somehow get to her—"

"We?" interrupted the minotaur.

I shrugged. "I mean, we both kind of screwed up here. I figure the least we could do is help each other out."

The minotaur considered me for a moment then nodded with an approving snort. "Perhaps *all* wizards aren't *all* bad."

I guess that was an apology, maybe?

"But it's too dangerous," he finished.

"We can take him."

"It's not about a fight. It's about Ceela. Jinns are shifty.

Ethereal air and fire. If we attack his lair, what's to stop him from hurting the principesse? No, there is another way."

I crossed my arms. "I'm all ears."

"Deal with them. This wizard promised Ceela wouldn't get hurt if you backed away. Give them what they want, Cisco. Do what they say. It's the only way to guarantee Ceela's safety."

Well, crap. I tried to look as apologetic as possible for this next part. "There's a problem, Throok. We can't deal. The information Simon doesn't want to get out? I already leaked it to my source." I swallowed, hoping not to enrage the monster. "It's too late to stop it."

He snarled. "That means we don't have time to argue. We need to get to them quick. Before the scandal goes public."

I nodded. "Except we don't have a boat or a jet. I know a lady. I could scrounge up more cash—"

"There's no time," said Throok. "You said this island is in the Caribbean?"

I pulled it up on Kita's phone. "Sure, along the underwater Sierra Maestras."

The minotaur's face flashed with recognition. "This jinn. Is he an ifrit?"

"How would I know?"

"He would command fire as your friend did lightning."

I frowned. "I've never seen him fight, but he melted through a steel chain like it was butter."

Throok grinned. "He's an ifrit. Very powerful. Very nasty."

"Then why are you smiling like a kid with a cookie?"

"Because I know the island you speak of. And I can get us there."

I didn't hide my surprise. "Is this some kind of Wonder Woman invisible jet thing?"

He growled. Silvans weren't big on pop culture.

"There's a reason Ceela and I chose this location to hide, wizard." The minotaur gazed at the sea again, this time pointing to a slight disturbance on the surface. A faint swirling of waves formed a barely-recognizable whirlpool. "At any moment, had Orpheus shown up, we had an escape route."

I stared into the deep. A section of water below the disturbance was darker. It was a rabbit hole.

Throok saw the look on my face. "Too late to back out now, wizard. Your speech about uniting our causes moved me."

"It wasn't really a speech," I backpedaled. "Just a few words, really."

The minotaur picked me up and heaved me into the ocean. I splashed through the surface and spun around, feeling less resistance than I should have, like I wasn't in water at all. I shot down through the portal, losing my grip on Kita's phone.

Next thing I knew, I slammed face-first into a dirt surface. I was underground now. Roots hung from the dirt above, with no visible exit.

I examined my crusted black hand. Great. A one-way trip to the Nether. The one place I *really* didn't want to be.

Chapter 31

The Margins of the Nether connect to all sorts of places in the world, rabbit holes with little sense or purpose, but useful. If Throok was right, getting to Connor's island was as simple as a stroll down a tunnel. Winding, twisting, indirect perhaps, but sometimes those make the best shortcuts.

I barely rolled out of the way as the minotaur's hooves thumped to the ground.

"Jeez," I said, looking up to him while on my back. "How do you guys manage that so gracefully?"

We were in a wide passage that stretched to forever in two directions. Spooky, maybe, but it felt comfortable with the darkness blanketing me. Like most of the Nether, I couldn't quite tell where the ambient light came from, but there was more than enough shadow to go around.

"By the way," I said, "thanks for the warning. I dropped the phone with the GPS coordinates."

Throok started down the tunnel. "I don't need it. We're

going to Fire Island."

"Isn't that a board game or something?"

He snorted. I liked to think I was wearing him down.

The silvan seemed to know the way to the aptly-named hunk of rock in the Caribbean. Every time the tunnel branched, he chose a route without hesitation. I followed silently, using the time to inventory my spellcraft tokens. My belt pouch was pretty light. I'd nearly gone through two weeks of nonstop preparation in the Everglades. I loaded my very last shotgun shell, another non-lethal glue round. This underground raid basically came down to me hoping Connor's compound wasn't well lit.

"So..." I said, breaking a long silence after more walking, "Connor's an ifrit, huh? What does that mean?"

Throok shrugged. "They wield fire. But you're a wizard. You can stop fire, I think."

I didn't want to shatter his high image of me. "Do ifrits have a weakness? Or jinns in general? I don't actually know a whole lot about them."

"There is a reason your kind speaks little of them," said the minotaur. "Ignorance against the jinn is powerful."

I arched an eyebrow. "Shouldn't it be the other way around?"

"Not in this case. You've met Orpheus, right? Fauns are fabled tricksters among your people, and mine. But jinns go beyond that. Every story of a jinn interacting with a human or silvan is a cautionary tale. Every one."

The ground got rockier and I had to watch each step or risk falling. "Cautionary how?"

Throok adeptly handled the terrain without looking. "Their deals are tainted. Jinns will appear to offer you the world, but it is part of their snare. They will lock you away if they can." He looked me in the eye. "Never deal with a jinn, wizard. It always ends in misery."

As we made our way through the tunnel, chitinous things peeked out at us. More than once I spun around to scurrying noises, but everything kept out of sight (even to my shadow-sharpened eyes).

"So how does this curse thing work?" I asked after a time. "Does every single thing down here hate me?"

Throok didn't slow his stride. "More or less."

"That's bad news because Orpheus has a whole spriggan army."

The minotaur grunted. "We don't need to worry about spriggans. They're underlings as far as fiends go. Weak, cowardly creatures, practically scared of their own shadow. They can be deadly en masse but, army or not, they stay alive because they're afraid of dangerous things. They don't leave the Nether. They don't face other armies head on. And they *never* attack someone with a Nether mark."

I flexed my stained hand. "Why not? I thought that was the whole point."

"Black marks aren't given lightly, wizard. Only awarded by royalty. Only to a worthy foe. To wear the black mark is a badge of honor in some circles. The spriggans revere that badge and won't dare attack a marked one for fear of being outmatched." Throok turned to me. "In a sense, under these circumstances, you're lucky to have it."

I chuckled. "Yeah," I said, deadpan. "I should play the lottery."

I stopped to shake a rock from my boot. Throok walked ahead, and I hissed.

"Lucky."

A black lump fell out of the upturned alligator hide. It wasn't a rock; it was a spider.

I kicked it away and jumped on one foot as it touched my sock. I backed against the wall and shoved my foot into my boot. The spider and I stood still, waiting for the other to make the first move.

Ahead, Throok paused, giving me an odd look. That's when I felt the appendage on my neck.

I screamed and shivered away, blasting through the shadow and into the far wall. I materialized pointing my shotgun at a large, eight-legged, one-foot-wide arachnid.

"Why's it always gotta be spiders?" I asked whoever was listening. There had to be somebody because this was too cruel to be a coincidence.

The thing wiggled its front legs like it was casting a spell, then suddenly broke loose from the wall and landed on the floor. I jerked my gun down, keeping a lock on it. Before I could pull the trigger, Throok's kukri came down and cleaved the thing in half. The minotaur kicked at the giant spider with his hoof. It was beyond dead.

I heaved out a frantic breath and lowered my weapon. "What?" I asked under his judgmental glare. "I *hate* spiders. I thought that would be an emotion you could empathize with."

Throok snorted and shook his head.

"Besides," I added, "what happened to things being too scared to attack me?"

He shrugged. "Scourgelings are little more than animals. They do not act out of desire for wealth or favor. To some of them, the black mark is a scent. An irritation. They have a natural drive to defend themselves against you no matter the danger. Spriggans are dumb, but they're not *that* dumb."

I shook my head. Keeping up with Nether ecology was a rollercoaster of ignorance.

"Were you really going to shoot a spider with a shotgun?"

I tilted my head. "It was a big spider."

With a dismissive breath, he mumbled, "As long as you have the ammo to waste."

I thought it would've been a perfectly reasonable use of my last shell, actually. I pushed off the wall. Something wriggled and jiggled and tickled my shoulder. I brushed at it.

More spiders. Suddenly the entire wall was crawling with them.

"This..." said Throok, his voice trailing off, "is abnormal."

"You don't happen to have a can of gasoline handy?"

"No, but I'm not afraid of getting messy." Still he was making fun of me.

"No need," I said, reaching into my belt pouch. "I have loose sparking powder. I can burn them all."

"No!" came a voice near us.

Throok and I whirled around. Standing fifty feet ahead, somehow, was Grettle, the brittle black-haired woman wearing a nightgown I'd seen last time I was in the Nether.

"Stand back," commanded Throok, approaching the girl. I wasn't sure if he was talking to me or her.

"It's okay," I said.

"She's with Orpheus. He found us."

"No," I said, pulling him back. I crept forward and studied Grettle's face. She still had the sadness from before, but her jaw was set and her eyes were determined. "I think she escaped." I approached her slowly. "What are you doing here?" I asked.

She eyed me with a quiet grin and wrapped her arms around her lanky figure. I couldn't help but feel sorry for her. Being so dirty and malnourished was awful, but somehow her happiness made it worse.

I tried again. "Do you need help, Grettle?"

She relaxed her head and whisked her tattered hair to the side. She wore a corset over her nightgown, and she reached her hands behind her, ripped it off, and threw it to the floor.

"I'm not the one surrounded by spiders," she said, then unfolded an extra pair of arms from behind her.

I took a step backward as Grettle's skin turned mottled gray. Her eyes swelled with pus and grew to half the size of her face, and her cheeks opened up into articulated mandibles. Finally, if that wasn't horrific enough, one of her four arms reached down and lifted her dress up. Between two grungy legs with bare feet hung another pair of legs, smaller and weaker than the main ones, toes dragging awkwardly in the dirt.

I looked up at whoever I was addressing before. "Now you're just fucking with me."

Chapter 32

Grettle screeched as she completed her transformation. The tips of her fingers had elongated into stiff claws that she now raked at me. I shifted through the shadow and, thankfully, phased through her attack.

Throok shot past me in a flash and swiped his kukri. Grettle nimbly jumped free and landed upside down on the ceiling. Oh, good. More creepy.

Even worse, she was right. Throok and I were literally surrounded by hundreds of spiders. The ground thickened with scurrying carapaces. I stomped them with my boots so much that their black blood dulled the shiny red alligator hide, and still they kept coming.

Throok engaged the woman, if you could still call her that. She had long arms for her size, but it was hard for anybody to get through a minotaur's reach. He was fast with his weapon and they kept each other at bay.

Instead of risking the shotgun, I withdrew the last of my bone dust. Just two snake fangs. It wasn't as formidable as before, but I didn't need to deal with an army this time. I clapped the powder between my hands and tossed the teeth to the floor. Two deadly cottonmouth spirits formed from shadows in the cloud.

Throok saw my spell. He battered Grettle, forcing her into the dust. The snakes lashed at her with ethereal teeth. She spun, having trouble both swiping them away and fending off Throok's attacks.

A chitinous whisper escaped her mandibles as she waved her hand in a cantrip. The spiders crowding me jumped for her. Some blanketed her back like living armor. Others dove at the ghostly water moccasins. The spiders couldn't latch onto the spirits, but their swipes and bites did scratch at my magic.

Even then, arachnids rushed past my feet. Large ones, tiny ones, raising their height like a flood. The creatures moved to smother my snakes completely.

Grettle, meanwhile, skittered away on the wall, waving one of her four arms and commanding her swarm.

She wasn't just a creepy silvan. She was a spider witch.

My snake magic was too weak to be much threat to the magically inclined. They were a terrifying display, but they mostly drew their power from fear, inflicting real damage after it was imagined. On the other hand, Grettle had an *actual* swarm of *actual* creatures. The spiders fell one by one, swallowed whole or split apart by razor-sharp fangs, but there were simply too many of them.

"Fire," I said, reaching for my spark powder.

Throok screamed as Grettle sliced his arm open, forcing

him to drop his blade. Grettle wrapped him up in a bear hug. Okay, a spider hug.

The minotaur wrested himself from her lanky arms, but she pulled him to the floor. They tumbled together, each vying for a superior position. One of my defining rules in life is to never grapple with a minotaur. Considering Grettle had twice as many arms and legs as he did, she had a better chance than most.

She scratched and clawed at his soft flesh, but even without his kukri, Throok had natural weapons himself. A horn gouged into her shoulder as she bit his arm. Between their screams and the legion of spiders crawling around me, I had plenty of motivation to end this quickly.

One of my snakes dissolved in a hiss. The other was in its dying throes. Some of the spiders split off to handle me. I threw the orange powder wide and spun in a circle, blanketing dirt, spider, and snake alike. Dozens of tiny mandibles chewed at my skin as I kneeled and sparked the lighter in my hand.

Flames roared to life all around me, immediately consuming the tunnel from ceiling to floor. I tried to hop through the shadow but, as the fire exploded brightly, I was tugged into the light. My magic had only bought me a second of relief.

Heat scorched my skin, instantly killing the biting spiders even before they visibly exploded. My shirt caught fire and my enhanced skin began to blister.

Nothing for it but to barrel out of the flames and plunge myself into the darkness. When I did, the live fire on me snuffed out. I phased back to the physical world on my hands and knees, breathing heavily and smoking like a giant block of dry ice. I felt worse than I looked.

Grettle wailed. Throok and the witch were well clear of the inferno, but her body shuddered as if she were burning alive. She had some kind of empathic bond with her pets. The minotaur rolled away from her. Grettle moved to regain her hold but Throok deftly scooped up his kukri and cleaved one of her hands off.

She screeched, again escaping to the ceiling, swollen eyes giving her spiderlings one last look. Then she sped down a tunnel offshoot I hadn't noticed before.

I wiped my face. The spiders were just a bunch of charcoal briquettes now. The last one left had just scurried away, missing a hand. I checked the side tunnel, but Throok grabbed me.

"No!" he boomed.

"She's wounded. We should take her now."

"No," he repeated, grabbing me by both shoulders. "Ceela's the priority. And she's this way." The minotaur headed down the wide tunnel.

I looked after Grettle with distaste in my mouth. I was leaving behind too many loose ends. Loose ends that would bite me in the ass the first chance they got. But Throok was right. Ceela was somebody else's loose end, and we needed to make sure she was safe before they took care of her.

We charged forward. The minotaur's pace made it clear we were only minutes away. Or maybe it had to do with the creatures following us.

"The spriggans," I warned. "They're behind us."

"They won't engage. They fear the black mark."

"But Grettle and the spriggans... Orpheus must be near."

He nodded and pointed ahead. "There! The rabbit hole!"

We raced to the portal. It was a circle of sand in the wall, its tan color a stark contrast to the dull brown dirt. An ancient glyph I didn't recognize was traced into the sand with edges sharp enough to be stone. Somehow, even though the filled-up opening was facing down at an angle, the sand didn't fall out. But then, rabbit holes tend to break the rules of physics.

"Damn it," said Throok, scraping his fingers against the hardened sand.

"What is it? What does it say?"

"I do not know the magic, but this is a Nether gate." Throok grumbled and lowered his head. "I *hate* Nether gates."

I rolled my eyes. "There has to be a way to break it," I said, reaching for the surface. "Anything that can be created can be destroyed."

"You don't need to," said the minotaur.

My hand passed through the sand with ease. As with the whirlpool, I could feel the sand but it was less viscous than it should've been. "What the..."

"This is a powerful defensive ward," he explained. "It will keep any and all Nether creatures at bay, silvan and scourgeling alike. But it's not made for your kind. You can pass through the gate freely."

Ravenous yells echoed in the passage behind us.

Throok lowered his head and spoke with a whisper. "You *must* pass through the gate."

I checked the tunnel, unnerved by the clanging noises. "But—"

"There's no time," he said. "The principesse needs our assistance now. You can provide that. I cannot."

I chewed my lip. "Without the black mark, the spriggans will close in on you. It's too dangerous."

He snorted impatiently. "I would gladly give my life for Ceela's. If this is how it must be done, so be it. You must save her. The Juniper Circle needs their principesse. *Nothing* else matters."

I could almost see his heart beating through his chest. His passion for her was intense. It made me think about the people I once loved. What I would do for them. Anything and everything, including sacrificing myself.

But there had to be another way.

"You won't be able to unravel the glyph," I told him, tracing my finger over it, searching for a way to nullify the ward. "Once I go through this gate, you'll be alone, unable to open the door."

Throok placed his hand on my shoulder. "Then make it count, wizard."

As I should have anticipated, he hefted me through the rabbit hole.

Chapter 33

I crawled out of a crabhole sheltered under a large rock on a sandy beach. It was still night. Rolling waves whisked over the shore and receded in a lazy rhythm, reflecting the stars above. The small island had a skirt of beach around it before breaking into hedges and palm trees. Dense vegetation took up half the land, shading an inlet, dock, and probably an airstrip. The other half of the island had been cleared for an elaborate mansion.

Columns made of stone supported a roof over a huge veranda entrance sandwiched by a pair of hexagonal gazebos larger than most houses. Behind that facade, the house rose above its two stories in various towers and viewing decks that opened to miles and miles of open sea.

Pizza delivery must've been expensive, but I was pretty sure Connor could afford it.

I triple-checked the coastline for more waterborne silvan surprises, but no mermaid would approach this island. This was a jinn stronghold, an Earthly base for something that didn't belong here.

I'd never seen a compound without walls before. You expect a drug lord to employ outposts and razor wire, but it was a clear fifty yards from the water to the beach to the framed lawn to the veranda. The windows were open glass. I didn't see a hint of security staff. Nothing at all was protected. Something told me the doors weren't even locked.

Halfway through deciding how to sneak in, I stood in the open, wiped the sand off my clothes, and walked right up to the front door. I opened it without a knock.

A black gentleman in a white suit held a silver tray to me, offering a glass of champagne. I waved off the offer. He nodded with a smile then beckoned me to follow. I guess I was expected.

We walked through the center hall of wide stone tiles. Modern electrical lights were recessed in the ceiling, but none of them were on. Instead, a combination of freestanding and wall sconces were outfitted with long, burning candles.

Right. Ifrit.

We entered a spacious hexagonal living area with mile-high windows. The view must've been amazing during the day. For now the scene they framed was black, mirroring the candlelight within. Low couches and pillows of every fabric and color littered the room like an opium den. Bookcases lined the walls. Low display cases contained arcane items, each dramatically lit: a cracked obsidian mask, a Taíno zemi, a half-burnt effigy of a multi-headed god.

There were larger presentations as well. Tall china cabinets with various ornaments and statues, crude weapons and flags hanging on the upper walls—this room was designed to impress.

At the window was a table of colored glass and ornate metalwork. It felt small compared to the rest of the room. Sitting casually with his legs crossed, swiping his cell phone on his lap, was Connor Hatch. He spoke without looking up.

"Is the light okay? I've always been more comfortable with the old ways."

He was letting me know he was a powerful being, much older than me. I didn't answer and approached the table.

"You humans and your electricity," he said, still tapping his phone. "I'd always seen it as such a waste. Instead of tapping into the Intrinsics, you capture energy from heat, of all things. How inefficient. But then I see curiosities like this. Computers. Software. It will be a magic of its own soon enough."

I stood at the chair across from him but didn't sit. He was playing Candy Crush. You gotta be a confident motherfucker to play a color-matching puzzle game while talking to someone who wants to kill you.

"Magic," I said. "Like a genie's wish?"

He finally turned to me. "Please don't use that word."

"Is it offensive?"

"No, it just makes you look like an idiot. But at least you know what I am, so you're not completely ignorant."

"First time for everything."

He smiled and returned his attention to his phone. "As a people, we're not supposed to cherish physical items. Really. It's one of our defining characteristics. Jinns don't hoard treasure. Rather, we value the intangible. Bonds of trust. Bargains. That sort of thing. More ephemeral, perhaps, but much more valuable."

I arched my neck, looking around the room. "I dunno. Looks like you've got a bunch of stuff to me."

The jinn chuckled. "True. The Aether is a place of spiritual being, but I count myself among those who indulge in Earthly pleasures. I wouldn't have created this empire otherwise."

I wasn't sure if I was supposed to be impressed.

Connor turned the screen off and set his phone on the glass. "I'm glad you're here. Do you need anything? Champagne? A glass of wine?" He studied me and leaned forward. "A Quesalupa Crunch Supreme?"

Whatever that last one was, it sounded good, but I shook my head firmly.

The jinn waved his hand and the man with the silver tray bowed and left the room, closing the double doors behind him.

"You see that?" asked Connor with pride. "Service. Another ephemeral treasure. Nothing says trust and loyalty like serving another, no matter your personal beliefs. Your kind used to value the same in the time of kings. But now humans have perverted the concept of service. What was once a pure ideal is now looked down on, seen as menial labor. No longer is working a noble pursuit. Now it comes with a price tag."

I shrugged. "Unions."

I wanted to use my shadow sight, to scan the room and look over the artifacts on display for a threat, but there was too much candlelight in here. I'd blind myself. While Connor was still reflecting on the virtues of butlers, I blew out the nearest wall sconce.

He turned to me with a curious expression.

"Where's the princess?" I asked heavily.

"Princess? That explains a few things." He relaxed and took a sip of champagne. "It is funny, don't you think, that a mongrel race such as the silvans presume to have royalty."

"So says the exalted drug peddler. Or is it extortionist? Killer, maybe?"

He shrugged casually. "You don't look like the type of person who likes to bullshit, so I'll be straight with you. I do a little of everything. And business is always expanding."

"Your money and bravado might be a force in the Caribbean, but how far do you think that will fly in the States?"

"That's what the Society is for," he answered. "They're a Yankee organization. Besides, the United States are floundering. An oversized country with a morality complex. One hand slapping the other. Tell me the truth, if you lived on an island like this, would you give a shit about the United States?"

"You want this little island? Fine." I took a step toward him. "But Miami's mine."

"I'm sure we could share."

"Where's the princess?"

He sighed. "Here. Clearly."

I strolled away from him, walking along the windows, studying everything I could. He was up to something.

"I don't know what your interest is in her," he continued. "But we can come to terms and you can have her, unharmed." He checked his phone and I blew out another set of candles.

"And Simon?" I asked, turning back to him.

"The wizard's long gone. He delivered my insurance and left me to watch over it. His people don't like confrontations."

"Could've fooled me. Though he certainly ran fast." I walked past a china cabinet. Glass shelves held a cigar box, a crystal sphere, a bowl of sparkling rocks, and other valuables.

"Yes," said Connor. "Once Simon saw how formidable you were, he rethought the Society's stance on you." The jinn smiled. "Don't think that means they forgot about you, Cisco. That just means they're holding back. Pooling their resources. And frankly, waiting to see how I deal with you first." He leaned forward. "You'll notice I haven't run."

I turned to him with a raised eyebrow. "So you don't lead the cartel then?"

"Cartel?" he said, laughing. "You mean the Society? I like that. But no. I don't lead them. I have my own cartel to worry about. They call it *Agua Fuego*, if you can believe that."

"Fire water."

He shrugged. "Latin America has a penchant for being literal, I'm afraid."

"So what does the Society want with the new Pablo Escobar?"

Connor smiled. "They're concerned American businessmen and politicians, all protecting each other's interests for the mutual good. I'm part of that mutual good. Businessmen do business, after all. You and I can do business, if you like."

He finished his champagne and I doused a large candle on a freestanding stick. Little by little, our corner of the room darkened.

The jinn leaned forward and said, "I'm just one link in that chain, Cisco. But make no mistake: I'm the strongest link. If you wanted to break their stranglehold, you came at the wrong person."

I stepped away from the smoking candle and shook my head. "I couldn't care less about the Society. This all begins and ends with you."

Connor rested back in his chair. "So said the seraphs when we three were created. But that wasn't quite true, was it?"

The jinn's cell phone chimed. I snuffed out another candle while he checked the screen. The corner of the room was now dim enough that I let darkness bleed into my irises.

Connor's phone rapped on the table. With my shadow sight, I saw a different aspect of the same man. His wild red hair was on fire. His beard hugged his chin in a warm glow, and his features seemed sharper than before. More volatile.

The charm on my eyes was far from able to see into other times or places. I couldn't see through magic or dispel illusions. I couldn't see beings in their true forms. The spellcraft simply reveals faint changes in the Intrinsics, the magical energies that govern the universe. So it surprised me that the jinn's aura was so stark. What had the Spaniard said? Jinns *are* magic.

His phone chimed again. "Excuse me," he said, annoyed now. He picked up his phone and I turned to the room.

The antiquities on display were historical, mostly, but some of them glowed with faint yellow and green hues, pregnant with enchantment. Those didn't concern me. What did were the threads of spellcraft hanging across the room like strings of lights—one leading to a doorway, another through a wall—strong lines of magic that faded and disappeared midair. Every single thread led to the cigar box in the China cabinet, where the glow was strongest.

Connor slammed his phone down again. "What is this?" he demanded. He looked around quizzically, then snapped his fingers. In an instant, every single candle I had doused roared to life.

I shook the black drops from my eyes and squinted at the man. His outward appearance was plain, but he was seething under the surface. Power thrummed around me. Every single open flame in the room leaned toward him.

"Something against light, Cisco? You aren't thinking of ambushing me once you've created enough shadow, are you?"

I showed my empty hands and shrugged. The truth was,

even full candlelight left me ample shadow to work with. I would just go without my shadow sight and be careful of my positioning. After a moment, the jinn relaxed and the candles idled normally.

He leaned forward. "You can't catch me, you know. The Aether is made of air and fire. I can disappear in a spark."

The jinn's phone chimed again, but he ignored it.

"Let's cut the pleasantries, human. Shall we talk terms?"

Terms. All I could think about were Throok's words. *Never deal with a jinn.*

He got another notification, quickly followed by another. He shook his head and checked his phone yet again. This time I noticed a slight intake of air.

"You may be a traditionalist, Connor, but this is the digital age. You can't just burn everything down with fire. Those were the old ways. Nowadays, everything leaves a footprint."

He swiped and tapped his phone with increasing agitation. I fell in by his side and read "Breaking News" across the screen. "City Scandal." Connor played a video from a news site and the tinny audio came through the speakers. "Lieutenant Cross came forward after, and I quote, 'undeniable evidence came to his attention.' The full scope of the scandal is still being realized, but City Commissioner Rudi Alvarez, a favorite for the mayor's office, is being sought for questioning."

Whoa. This was moving much faster than I thought possible.

Connor pounded his phone onto the table so hard a web

of cracks splintered the glass surface. He lifted his head and the rage was finally evident, eyes burning like the surrounding candles.

"What. Have. You. Done?" he growled.

Chapter 34

Despite his anger, Connor surprised me. He kept his seat. It was the sign of a measured being. Of someone old and patient.

Cisco Suarez didn't have those traits. I goaded him on. "I'm afraid you can't buy yourself out of this mess."

"Please," he replied with renewed calm. "Everything has a price. Everyone has something they want. Even you."

"You think I'm gonna deal with you?" I laughed harshly. "You had me killed!"

"I never gave that order."

"Don't talk to me about personal autonomy. You set the Covey loose in Miami to wreak havoc. The blame for the fallout is yours. Because of you, everything I loved is gone."

The jinn sighed. "To be honest, Tunji was overeager. His ruthlessness is what made him effective, but he no doubt created enemies in the process. You're one I would take back."

"You had ten years of zombie service to object to my

treatment. But this isn't about that fiend. When a shoddily-built house falls to a hurricane, you don't blame the guy who slapped up the drywall. You blame the architect. This whole shadow play was yours from the beginning." The darkness gathered around me, fighting the candlelight. It cloaked my fist like a boxing glove. "You need to answer for that."

I saw the resolve leave Connor's face. He knew it was a lost cause, that we would come to blows. This wasn't a wound that could be patched up. Yet he was still sitting. I couldn't figure out what he was playing at.

"The little shadow witch," he mused. "You forget that you are human and I am jinn."

"Equals to the seraphs."

"Not equals. Not even close. You could throw your spell, and within a blink I'd be gone. I can vanish and leave you to enjoy the comforts of the Caribbean alone."

I took a confident step forward. "But then you lose the princess. You can run to the Aether with your tail between your legs, but you can't take anyone or anything with you."

He flashed a wry smile. "Too true. Then again, I no longer care about the princess. She wasn't my play. The damage to the politician is done. You can have her."

He beckoned with his hand and a door across the room opened. Ceela stood within, eyes red, hands bound with duct tape. Her aimless gaze drifted past me and focused on nothing in particular.

My head swiveled between them. The jinn did nothing but watch.

"Let us talk then," he said, "about what it is you want. The silvan is only the start. Is it the city commissioner? The Covey? What does your heart desire, Cisco?"

I ignored Connor and approached the satyr carefully. I paused when I noticed the black man in the white suit behind her. He put his hand around her waist and walked her inside the room. Then he respectfully bowed back to the doorway, watching.

"Are you okay, Ceela?"

Her head sagged to face the floor. She blinked slowly as if she were drugged.

"Can you hear me?"

Connor stood for the first time, coming to my side, but still using his phone to browse the news outlets. "Come now, Cisco. She'll be all right."

I turned to him with daggers in my eyes. "What did you do to her?"

He took a deep breath in preparation of a smug answer. Before he got a word out, my fist rocketed into him. The shadow tightened and compressed with the blow, black and unyielding.

Connor disappeared.

His phone plopped to the ground at my feet, but that was all that was left. His clothes were fake, part of him, as with silvans.

"You think this is a boxing match?" he chuckled from behind me.

I spun around and swung at him again. This time when he vanished I dipped into the shadow, sliding backward a few yards, materializing just as he did, him behind me then me behind him. My fist cracked into his back, but again connected with nothing but air.

Connor now stood beside Ceela. She tottered in place, threatening to topple at any moment. He was bent over at the waist, looking up at her face in amusement. "What do you suppose is going through her head right now?"

I lashed out at him with a spear of shadow. It stood erect on the floor like a porcupine's quill, impaling the spot where Connor's belly had been a moment before.

"This is getting tiresome," he yawned, leaning against the wall on the other side of the room.

I palmed my bronze knife and stomped toward him.

He didn't budge. "A knife now? You think your blade can find me where the shadow couldn't?"

"Hardly." I lashed it across my blackened palm. Blood oozed as I muttered a curse on my lips. My hand reached through him to the wall behind, and again the jinn was behind me.

"Enough of this," he snapped.

"Coward!" I screamed. "Why won't you fight me?"

I dug through my belt pouch. I'd come here out of desperation, ill prepared and out of time, but I had a few tributes left. I fingered a sack of powder. Not poison, really; its effects were disorienting, almost hallucinatory. If he was made of air, maybe I could pollute it.

I waved the sack at him. The dust hung in a mass, enveloping everything. It consumed Connor's form in a cloud. He didn't even vanish this time. Dust settled on glass display cases and the floor, but the jinn was unaffected.

His face went hard and his eyes burned. "I said *enough*!" he roared. Every candle in the room flared and he kicked over a vase in anger. It shattered to pieces, further setting him off.

I didn't let up. Something would hurt him. I just had to find it. I drew my shotgun from the shadows.

That made him even more livid. For a brief moment, Connor Hatch lost control. The jinn lumbered at me and raised his fist. And then... he stopped.

For a full minute, neither of us moved. Him with his fist drawn, me with my sawed off pointed at his head. I didn't fire because I realized it was a useless gesture. My glueshot would go right through him and I'd have wasted my last shell.

The question on *my* mind was, why was the *jinn* holding back?

I slowly lowered the shotgun, watching him seethe and huff and do his best to stare me down. Eventually he composed himself and he lowered his arm.

"You can't kill me," I realized. "Can you?"

Connor's eyes burned with ire and I knew I was right.

"Never deal with a jinn," I whispered, dropping my guard completely. "You have no power over me. As long as I don't enter a contract with you, you can't hurt me, can you, you son of a bitch?"

Composed now, Connor hiked a shoulder like it was inconsequential. "There are many ways I can have you killed."

"But you can't do it yourself."

He laughed. "You think that means I have no power?" He spun around, presenting the room to me. Ceela, the servant, his grand collection. It was all his. "Everything you see is power."

Connor put his hands in his pockets and walked through the room. "Our kind—some of our number were slaves once. To your people. These stories comprise the totality of what you know of the jinn. But this is barely a speck of sand in our realm."

I scraped my teeth into a scowl and stepped closer to him. "Yet here we are. Just you and me. How does it feel to be alone and helpless?"

He immediately turned to me with a devilish grin. "Is *that* it? You think we're alone?"

My grip on the shotgun tightened.

The jinn raised an arm in the air and called out, "Come."

The man in the white suit moved beside Connor. His skin cracked. Rivulets of orange light seeped through his flesh, setting his clothes alight and revealing rocky flesh below.

I knew this man. Not the face or the build. Not the skin I saw. But I knew the elemental underneath it: Tyson Roderick, Rudi Alvarez's former head of security.

Pieces of ash crumbled to the floor as the volcanic elemental assumed his true form. Molten lava flowed between plates of rockskin. He was another primal being from the Aether, pure magic taking form in the Earthly Steppe as elemental energy. And, for some reason, taking orders from a jinn.

Then another door in the hexagonal room opened. Kita Mariko strolled in, heels clicking against the floor until she joined the elemental. With a sly smile, she slipped her fan from her sleeve. The magical weapon elongated into a rudimentary sword.

So much for my advice to cut and run. The paper mage met my mercy with continuing contempt. The bloodlust was clear on her face.

This was it, then. In a way, everything I wanted. Tunji and the obeah man wouldn't be making an appearance 'cause they were dead. But Connor, Tyson, Kita...

"Well," I announced, impressed (and just a little bit scared). "If it isn't the Covey itself. All present and accounted for."

The jinn's smile grew wide. "No, Cisco, not yet. There is one other."

He snapped his fingers and a third door opened. My heart stopped beating. The next person to enter was Em.

Chapter 35

I surged forward but Kita moved in my way, forcing me to stop and look over her shoulder.

"Emily," I said frantically. My voice cracked and they heard it and I hated that. "What are you doing here?"

My ex wasn't the same as the others. She wasn't a primal being. She wasn't an animist or a Nether fiend. She was just a woman caught up in her sister's plot. There was no reason for her to be here.

"You speak of power," chimed Connor, puffing his chest out. "What, I ask you, is the most powerful and dangerous force in a sentient being?"

My eyes flicked from one person to the other. Besides Ceela and Emily, all I saw was hatred.

"Passion," said the jinn, answering his own question. "You can pay a soldier a fortune. You can threaten him with eternal suffering. But, to a man, each will fight harder and better if they *believe* in you. If they *love* you."

Connor lifted his finger. "Passion is what I inspire in my

Covey. It's what made you blind to Emily's advances ten years ago when she planted the seed in your head. She invisibly guided you—made you believe it was you who wanted to find the Horn."

I stared at my ex, wordlessly imploring her to do something—to say something. She held her lips taut and avoided meeting my gaze.

I frowned. My finger lightly rubbed the trigger of my sawed off, but I held it down, at my side. The jinn reveled in my hesitation.

"Passion is nature," he continued. "Passion stirs us to do incredible things. Brains control reason, but hearts veto logic every time. The excitement of discovery, the drive to create, the urge to kill..." Connor strolled to Emily and laid a gentle hand on her shoulder. "Even the desire for affection. You remember that passion, don't you? I bet it still nips at you."

The smug son of a bitch. I worked my jaw, wondering how I could break his.

"What about you, darling?" The jinn moved to Ceela and leaned into her. She flinched at his touch, but didn't retreat. "Ah, this one needs more time." His finger traced her cheek and ran down her neck, right past her heart locket.

Her.

Heart.

Locket.

My eyes darted to Emily. She had the same locket. Kita and Tyson had bare necks, but Emily and Ceela wore lockets. Suddenly Emily's inconsistent behavior made sense. She'd betrayed me but named Fran after me. She was sorry for what happened to my family, and hers I think, yet she continued to operate within the organization responsible. The conflicting emotions made sense because she was in a conflict. Fighting. Trapped. Just like Ceela.

I snuffed out the closest candle with my palm, keeping my hand on the hot wax so the jinn couldn't rekindle it. My eyes pulled in the shadow again.

"Give me light!" boomed Connor, and the flames swelled.

A white brilliance flooded the room. It was much brighter than before. Like looking at the sun, and it hurt twice as much. I strained to see through the glare anyway, but it was no use. From this distance, it was impossible to inspect the lockets.

My eyes burned and the shadow began to dry up. Then Ceela moved. It wasn't much, just a quick stumble to the side. Connor laughed and let her go, but it wasn't important. The movement was. Even with my fading shadow sight and the white haze obscuring my vision, that sharp movement drew my eye to something I'd seen earlier.

A red twine of magic leading to Ceela.

I flushed my eyes and blinked. I was blind. Hoping I had a good poker face, I rubbed my eyes casually and stood in place.

But my mind was moving a mile a minute.

"Why are you still here?" I posed, more to myself than the others.

The jinn's light footsteps returned to his position between Kita and Tyson. "Hmm?"

I wet my lips as I worked it out. "If you can blink out, return to the Aether in a flash, what are you still doing here? Why confront me at all?" Vague hazes of light swam in my face.

"Why not?" Connor answered. "You can't hurt me."

"It's because you're a collector." I waved my shotgun across the room as I started making out smudges of color again. "You collect valuables. Antiquities. Even people."

A smile played across Connor's face. "Like baseball cards."

"Or maybe it's something else." I nodded, my expression weighing the riddle. "Maybe it has something to do with what's in the cigar box over there?"

The air in the room went still, and the jinn's smile faltered.

"For a long time," I explained, "I was a thrall to the vampire's compulsions and the obeah man's spellcraft. Ten years of my life, not only wasted, but upheaved. So I know something about service." I saw how frightened Ceela was. I saw the pain in Emily's eyes. "How many others have been similar victims?"

Connor snorted. "You misunderstand. The vampire's methods were crude. I do not numb the mind. I merely whisper to it. Those who follow me respect the revolution. They feel the winds of change blowing."

I smiled. "The winds of change, huh?"

"Every revolution starts with a single insurgent."

"Isn't that right," I agreed, and raised my shotgun to the China cabinet.

Connor didn't have time to give orders, or to even shout. In a flash, he appeared between me and my target.

I pulled the trigger and the gun barked, sending a spread of glue in a wide cone. Connor vanished and the glass display shattered, rocking the entire case back into the wall. The three shelves below the cigar box were a gooey mess, but my aim had accomplished what I wanted. I charged the cabinet and ripped open the cigar box with ease.

The prize in this particular cereal box was a multi-faceted ruby heart. It was weighty, the size of a small fist, etched with writing I didn't have time to make out. I knew an artifact when I held one.

So the genie had a lamp.

Except this lamp enslaved *other* people. Not with a compulsion, but by stirring their souls. By making them believe they were doing the right thing. This artifact, whatever it was, hooked heart strings to helpless victims, each wearing a locket as an anchor.

I rubbed the scratch on my neck and imagined the scar on my heart. The heart locket. That was what Simon had tried to use on me. Why I'd been so dazed back there. It was also how Simon had kidnapped satyr royalty so effortlessly. The jinn couldn't directly attack us himself so he'd used trusted animists to do it. Simon for me. Kita for Emily.

I knew Emily had been the privileged one. Henry Hoover's only child from his wife. The one who traveled the world instead of being left behind. Just as Kita had always hated her father, she'd condemned her own sister too.

Each passing second drew a different tragedy to my mind. All the ills caused by a single gemstone. My knuckles went white as my grip on the artifact tightened.

"Get the heartstone!" yelled the jinn.

Kita immediately flanked me and brandished her fan. The elemental inhaled a long gulp of air, and I knew what was coming next. I'd seen his lava magic before—had a similar problem with Simon's lightning. Both Intrinsics created light, disrupted my shadow, and stung like a bitch.

The room was still bright. Unless my eyes hadn't fully recovered, the orange flames had somehow swallowed much of the available shadow. It weakened me, no doubt, but there was enough darkness to play with. As long as I was careful.

"This is where we're different," I taunted Connor. "I can take things with me."

A river of lava spewed from Tyson's mouth. I used the shadow, not to become ethereal, but for speed, darting out of the way of the molten liquid. It steamed and melted the glass behind me.

I slipped behind Kita with the same dash. I readied a shadow punch but she was faster, kicking a leg behind her and catching me in the gut. I doubled over and dropped the heartstone to the floor.

I reached for it but Kita's extended fan blade came down. I dove to the side and swept my boot into her legs, sending her tumbling.

"Don't do this," I urged. "Don't betray your sister."

We both scrambled to the heart but I was faster. I slithered forward in the darkness and scooped it up.

"More light!" bellowed Connor. "I want more light!"

A hand wave from the jinn sent all the candles in the room into overdrive, burning three times brighter than should've been possible. But he wasn't the real source of light. Another animist stepped forward and I just now noticed her raised hand, fingers clawed around an orb of pure incandescence.

I choked up. "Em?"

My ex-girlfriend avoided my gaze and held her hand high. The light was coming from her. The shadows cowered from the brilliance, drying up my playground with blinding white radiance.

Blind indeed. That's what I'd been.

Emily Cross was an animist.

Kita pulled a backwards somersault and vaulted to her feet. In the small opening, the volcanic elemental came for me, igneous rock shaking the floor as he stomped. But the paper mage held up an open palm.

"He's mine!" she snarled, licking her lips. "Keep the light on him."

Still on the floor, I gripped the ruby heart in both hands, drew it above my head, and slammed it down hard. It nearly bounced out of my grasp, still intact.

Kita came at me with a feint and a swipe. Her fan moved so fast it left tracers of yellow in the air. There was too much light. I kicked a sconce at her. The fan sliced it in half with ease. The candles dropped to the floor right next to me, flaring brighter.

"Smooth," I said to myself.

The paper mage spun on her heels, flipping her attack to the opposite side. I gritted my teeth for the pain I knew was coming and threw up my forearm. Right before the fan struck, she flicked the back half of it open.

The impact was blinding. Golden sparks met the protective turquoise of my armor. Power hopped between us. The force was explosive. Literally.

But Kita held her own, using the open portion of the fan as a shield. Instead of being forced back, she kept the edge of her weapon firmly planted on my armor tattoo, pressing down, both hands backed by her full weight.

The Intrinsics went crazy, fighting to complete their purpose, dazzling and cracking and popping and burning. I averted my eyes and pressed against the fan with everything I had, but she had leverage. She had light. She had a razor-sharp fan.

And it was cutting into my skin.

Chapter 36

I groaned under Kita's strength. Blood ran down my arm like water from an open faucet. I wiped my palm through the blood and clamped down on her wrist. The contact sizzled her flesh. Her eyes went wild, but she only pressed harder.

Her fan blade bit deeper into my arm. Right through my armor. Right through my zombie skin. Cutting to the bone. The pain was unbearable. Kita had to have been feeling something similar from my blood, but she was too close now. If this kept up, she'd slice clean through me.

"Do something," I grunted, turning to Em.

"Stay out of this, Emily," warned her sister.

Tears ran down Em's face now, but she didn't move. More conflicting behavior. Behind her, Ceela was barely aware of what was happening, fighting her own battle inside her head. The two men in the room, if you could call them that, stood eager. Tyson watched as one might the final seconds of a football game. And Connor Hatch was filled with awful glee.

A twanging pain raced up my left shoulder as I lost the feeling in my hand. My nerves were shot now. The shadow was gone. Still holding my forearm above my head, I released Kita's wrist and let the blood magic fall away. Then my free fist came up hard and fast into her belly.

Immediately, the force bearing down on me lessened. Kita's fierce demeanor was ever stubborn, but her eyes grew lazy. She furrowed her brow and stumbled backward.

I shoved away and hugged my wounded arm, securing the heartstone once more.

Kita Mariko coughed. The fan in her hands shrank down to normal size, and then it clattered to the floor, just bamboo and paper. Its golden aura winked out. The paper mage's hands clutched the ceremonial bronze knife protruding from her gut. Then she buckled to the floor.

Emily screamed and the bright light snuffed out. Tyson roared. My alligator boot kicked the candle on the floor away from me. Then I cupped both hands around the ruby heart and surrounded it with shadow.

"No!" screamed Connor. Emily kneeled by her sister. The elemental lumbered toward me.

Compressing shadow into something hard, something physical, is unnatural. To do it with the density I needed felt like fighting the pull of a black hole. But I was strong. I'd been around the block once or twice. I was at home in the shadow. And I needed this.

The orb of pure darkness attempted to escape my fingers. I squeezed harder. Once again gripping the heartstone, I let myself think of every single gross act that had been done in its name. Emily. Martine. My parents. My sister. I brought them all to bear on my conscience in an unrelenting weight.

And I shattered the hell out of that pansy artifact.

The ruby exploded, much of it impacting my chest and arms. The pain was nothing compared to what I already carried.

Connor's face was clear for one last, brief moment. He watched his entire house of cards topple. His empire, he called it. Service.

I didn't see nobility. I saw subjugation. Contempt. Panic. It was all etched into his sharp features.

And then he was gone.

Every candle in the mansion simultaneously winked out. The darkness encompassed us like a crypt.

Me? This was my element. It was more like a blanket.

I saw every detail as my eyes sucked in the black. Numerous heart strings flailed in the air. Without a power source, they withered and dissolved in seconds. In their absence, the Covey stood aimless. Confused. Ceela crumpled to the floor, exhausted.

I wasn't sure what would happen next. Destroying artifacts is a tricky business. The effort could easily have unintended results. But for their part, no one went into a rage and attacked me. With Connor gone, and his hold on them, they were purposeless.

I waited as their eyes adjusted to the faint light of the lava coursing through the volcanic elemental, and I wondered why he wasn't attacking me as well.

"Where am I?" choked out Kita. "Emily?"

I rose to my feet. "Oh no."

I hurried to the fallen paper mage. Blood spurted from her mouth and sprayed her older sister's face. Kita Mariko shuddered as she took painful breaths. I ran my hand under the collar of her jacket and felt the same neck I'd once held a knife to. It was bare, as I'd known.

"She's one of them," I swore.

"Emily?" asked Kita again, her eyes going distant, affixed to a far-off place. Em squeezed her sister's hand and leaned close.

"It's over, Kita," she said. "It's over."

Kita's body tightened and a final, racking breath fled her lips, and then she was gone.

I didn't know what to say as the sun crested over the horizon and filled the room with new light. The silence stretched into minutes.

"You killed her," whispered Emily.

She gripped her half sister's hand tightly, as if it were up to her whether she could let go or not. I almost spoke but a glint of light caught my eye. Around Kita's wrist was a thin bracelet with a heart-locket charm.

"You killed her," whispered Emily, once again.

"I didn't know," I offered weakly, clutching my bleeding arm. I backed away as Em refused to look at me. I'm not great with women, but I know when nothing I say could possibly help.

Ceela's human guise convulsed on the floor. I ran to the

girl and ripped the locket from her neck. Then I carefully unwrapped the duct tape binding her wrists.

"How do you feel?"

"Like a used toothbrush," she said, shivering.

"Throok and I came for you."

"Throok?" Confidence spread through her like a drug.

I nodded. "He couldn't get past the Nether gate. I..."

She read the gloom on my face. "We need to help him."

Damn it. She was right. We had to get out of here, anyway. I wrapped the length of duct tape around my forearm, grimacing as I pulled the wound tight to stem the bleeding. After I was done, the cut was completely covered and sealed. I was a bloody mess, but what hadn't already leaked should now stay inside.

I returned to Kita's body, picking up the knife that lay beside her. She was dead, no two ways about it. I softly placed my hands on Emily's shoulders. "We have to go."

She shook at my touch. "I'm not going anywhere."

"Wizard," urged Ceela, leaning on the doorway. "We need to hurry."

I ignored her. "We can't stay here, Em. Who knows when he'll be back? He might bring help."

"I'm *not* leaving my sister."

I hissed. I wanted to throw her over my shoulder and drag her out, kicking and screaming.

Two heavy feet stopped beside me. It was Tyson Roderick, returned to his human form, the man in the white suit. "I'll take them," he said, dropping a broken heart locket on the floor.

His voice wavered as he spoke. Even an elemental like himself had to deal with the after effects of being a thrall. I wasn't sure if I could trust him, if he cared for anything in the Earthly Steppe, but something told me he'd be true to his word.

They knew each other well, after all. They were the Covey. What was alive of them, anyway. Free, but broken. There had to be kinship there.

Emily's safety was my main concern, of course. Tyson or not, I didn't want to leave her. I leaned over to her once more, words ready on my lips to convince her to come with me.

She lashed out viciously. "I can't deal with you right now!"

I drew back.

"Wizard," reminded the satyr.

My eyes met the elemental's. I thought of Throok and cursed. I told Emily I'd be back, but I wasn't sure if it came out louder than a whisper. Then I hurried out of the hexagonal room.

Ceela was still disoriented from the heartstone's pull. Whatever its effects had been, she'd fought it, never fully tamed. I wondered how long the effects would take to completely wear off, if the Covey could ever truly recover.

I thought of Emily's inconsistent behavior. It was very likely Connor had to deal with times of greater and lesser control, when Emily could've almost escaped his clutches until he resparked her passion and returned her to the fold without question. Maybe, with the leash gone, they would all be free for good. Or maybe the pull on her heart would still be forever present. Control was a bitch like that.

Ceela had only been exposed for a short time. Her withdrawals were mostly physical; she was dizzy and weak. I helped her down the patio steps, but she was determined to walk on her own after that.

"There it is," I said, pointing to the crab hole. "Will you be able to get through?"

"It depends if he bothered to ward the gate going both ways."

I jumped in first, actually managing to land in the Nether on my knees this time. The effort pulled open the cut on my arm, though.

The welcome face of the minotaur greeted me. Throok watched as Ceela's hooves daintily hit solid ground beside me. Surrounding us was a horde of dead spriggans. Their bodies were crushed, trampled, beaten, and gored six ways from Sunday. For Throok's part, he looked pretty beat up himself, even if most of the blood on him wasn't his own.

"Throok!" shouted Ceela in glee. She ran and threw her arms around him.

Already, I thought, she looked stronger. Whether it was the Nether or her natural form, I knew the principesse would be fine in a day or two. Plenty of bed rest and whatever passed for chicken soup down here, she'd be good as new.

Throok was different, though. He remained in the same blunt pose as before, not returning the girl's embrace. She noticed it too. The satyr pulled away and eyed him strangely. And then I heard chitinous laughter.

Grettle sauntered out of a side passage, dragging her extra pair of dead legs underneath. She was still missing a hand, but twisted Throok's kukri in another. A third guided a length of shining string. No—a line of web. It pulled taut against the minotaur, binding his arms to his side.

The spider witch grinned, but it wasn't her that spoke.

"Like flies in a web," remarked Orpheus, emerging into the tunnel.

Chapter 37

Ceela recoiled from the minotaur. Throok's muscles rippled but his arms were bound to his sides. He attempted to step between the faun and the princess, but his legs were tied too. Without the satyr supporting his weight, he would've tripped.

"Orpheus," I grumbled, tightening the duct tape around my arm. "I've had a bad day."

"They'll get worse as the mark does," he rejoined. He tapped his boomerang against his curved horn. "But that's what you get for manhandling me, human."

"My hands are covered in blood. I could do it again."

Orpheus handed his weapon to Grettle. She took it with her last free hand and stood in my way, a bouncer preventing access to an exclusive silvan party. A bouncer with a sword, a boomerang-hatchet, a web, and a stump. Just to make the point that it wasn't a nice party, she pointed the kukri at me.

I assessed the situation. Throok was tied up. Ceela still

disoriented. Me? I'd live. My supply was cashed, but I still had blood and shadow. There was always plenty of that in the world. For now, I bided my time, waiting for an opening.

"Wizard," chided Orpheus. "This is Nether business. I am a baron of Bone, she a principesse of Juniper. Leave the politicking to us."

The faun stroked his scraggly beard as he rounded Throok. He ignored the larger silvan completely, turning all his attention on the object of his desire. A toothy grin overtook his goat face, and his pointed ears relaxed.

"There you are, my dear." His voice was soft now. Gentle. "Do not worry. I will not mistreat you." He took her hand in his. Grettle hissed lightly.

"Don't hurt him!" cried Ceela, her eyes watering.

The faun's brow furrowed. "Him? You are concerned for him?" Orpheus considered the minotaur and nodded. "Fine, my love. Whatever you ask. He shall be released when we depart."

Grettle spun to him, producing her stump hand. "He maimed me, my lord."

Orpheus sighed. "Yes. We will see what we can do about that."

"We can *eat* him," she insisted. "You told me I could have them both."

"No!" said Ceela, her thin chest heaving.

Orpheus tightened his lip and held out his hand. "My hatchet, dear."

Grettle smiled and placed the bone weapon in his hand.

The faun hefted the familiar weight and deftly snapped the web connecting the spider witch to her prey. Throok was still bound but no longer leashed. With the sudden absence of resistance, he lost his balance and fell on his shoulder.

"But Orpheus!" screeched the witch.

"I will not hear it!" he snapped. The witch shied away from his tone. "The principesse is my betrothed and I will respect her wishes." He turned to address Throok. "The bindings will dissolve in a short time. When they do, see that you do not follow us. The Circle of Bone would not welcome your presence."

Ceela watched Throok with shimmering doe eyes as the faun pulled her away. Grettle scoffed heartlessly as she towered over him. She looked me over, too, bulbous eyes filled with depravity and wickedness, mandibles salivating from her desire to eat my flesh.

"Come, my love," whispered Orpheus to Ceela, kneeling before her and kissing her hand.

Grettle turned, and all the hate festering in her eyes before was nothing compared to what surfaced now. A high-pitched cry seeped from her throat and filled the cavern. Then the spider witch lunged.

It was quick and dirty. A moment of unbridled passion and fury. Grettle lifted the kukri high and brought it down towards Ceela's turned head. Throok jerked in his bindings. I dove into shadow and dashed forward—but even I was too slow. I rematerialized behind the spider witch at the end of her blow.

Only her blow never landed. The kukri was flung wildly

and staked into the dirt. Grettle's arm was still attached, resting beside it. A large gash ran across her chest leading to the severed shoulder. Orpheus stood between his princess and his witch, hatchet held low, painted with black blood.

For a moment, the spider witch balanced on four legs. Then, as she folded to the floor, Orpheus caught her and laid her gently on her back.

Grettle's eyes shrank and her jaw closed, taking on her more human appearance. Pale, lanky, dirty. She spat out blood as she stared into the faun's face. "I..." she rasped, forcing her eyes to focus. "I do not blame you." Then her head went limp.

The baron closed her eyes and waited a long moment, shutting out the rest of the world. Out of a strange deference, no one moved.

"She loved me, you know," he said softly. "But I love another. And so it goes."

Ceela was white as a ghost, still jolted by her close call. Somehow she summoned the courage to speak. "You can't dictate the heart, Orpheus," she said compassionately, eyes trailing to Throok. When he met her gaze she seemed to grow taller, her conviction steadying. "Just as you love me, so too do I love another."

She knelt beside the minotaur and unraveled the weakening web. Throok ripped away the remnants and the two silvans kissed.

Orpheus waited until their embrace was done, rested his hand one last time on Grettle, and stood with a sigh. "You will dishonor the Oak Table with that wedding. Instead of forming a political alliance, you will foment a war."

The minotaur stood and puffed his chest out. He took a step forward and growled.

Ceela placed a dainty hand on his chest. "Love is a cause worth fighting for."

"And should I not as well?" returned Orpheus.

She shrugged. "If you wish. Just realize that the only one fomenting war is you."

I'd never realized how regal Ceela looked before. I mean, she was still a kid. She had a lot to learn, but I had no doubt she would learn it.

I retrieved Throok's sword and tossed it to him, mainly 'cause I felt pretty useless so far. He held it ready at his side. I was ready for anything too, but Orpheus was done fighting. He was outnumbered and introspective. His love for the satyr, if that's what it was, would never be returned. And now the one who *had* loved him was lost forever.

"You cannot win me," said Ceela. "You cannot earn me in time." The satyr's voice rose and I perked my ears at the oncoming silvan justice. "It was never about your status or exploits, Orpheus. It was about you, and me, and how we felt for each other. The best you can do is find a place beside us at the Oak Table."

Take that. I blinked. "Wait. You're gonna let this guy join you?"

She shrugged. "It's a smart alliance, Cisco. One that is clearly already desired by both circles. Besides, it comes with a price." The satyr turned to the faun baron. "Remove the curse on the wizard. Let him free. He was merely doing as I beseeched, and attacking him is like attacking myself."

Orpheus nodded glumly. "A day, a night. Consumed by blight. Come from the dark, free of the mark. It is done, human."

The black mark itched. The crust turned to dust and fell away. The discolored stain beneath shriveled until it was nothing. My hand, my skin, the tattoo—they were fine. Back to normal.

I shook my head. My life was an addendum to a silvan alliance. *This* is why I hate the Nether.

"We should get moving," said Throok, all business.

The principesse nodded and turned to me. "Will you accompany us to our dominion?"

"I..." I rubbed my face. "I can't. I have business on Fire Island. But you can't stick around down here with..." I pointed my eyes at Orpheus even though he could plainly see my face. He sighed loudly.

"Wait a minute," I complained, not willing to let this slide. "Is that it? We're supposed to pretend nothing happened? We all just shake hands and say our goodbyes?"

"Goodbyes," grumbled the minotaur in a dour voice. A grin hid beneath his snout as he offered his hand. "I *hate* goodbyes."

I answered his grip with mine. "The smile doesn't suit you, bud."

He grew serious. "Thanks for your service to the principesse."

Ceela stood on her tiptoes and kissed me on the cheek. "The Juniper Circle is grateful, wizard."

The young couple started down the tunnel. I waited. I told myself I was making sure Orpheus didn't trail them, but the truth was I didn't know what to do. My immediate concerns were handled and I was left feeling a little stunned. I stared at the new skin on my hand, wondering about fresh starts.

Orpheus whistled and several spriggans stomped from their passage, eyeing me warily. At his command, they lifted the spider witch's body and carried it away. Orpheus followed them, heavy of heart, parting words trailing behind him.

"The Nether mark is gone, wizard, but I cannot absolve you of the deaths on your hands. The mermaid, Gemma—she lusts for your blood. And I cannot dissuade her course."

"That much I understand," I said, Kita Mariko's dying face etched into my memory. "They're not the only pair of sisters I've broken up."

Chapter 38

Heartstrings are funny things. They pull at us when we least want them to. They hurt with little reason or recourse. We lock them under layers of pleasantries, pretend we're not damaged, and carry forward, but no matter our heads we can never cut them away completely.

Our hearts inspire us to take wild leaps and desperate gambits, often to our detriment. Some see wisdom in ignoring these pulls. One thing humankind may never learn is how to control where our strings lead.

Emily Cross was never evil. She'd been a thrall of sorts, under a compulsion of passion. Find Cisco Suarez, the Taíno shadow charmer. String him along until he discovers the Horn of Subjugation, the key to gaining a death grip on the Miami necromantic community. Plain and simple, Emily had marching orders and she executed them as she believed was right. As Connor Hatch had forced her to believe.

And I killed her sister for it.

The Covey were all victims, in a sense, used for their power, influence, and assets. Just like I had been. Maybe theirs wasn't a full compulsion, but a suggestion. A driving spirit. Perhaps they were seduced by powerful forces, tricked into compromises that ultimately surrendered their souls. But could I take the moral high ground? Could I claim that I hadn't searched for the Horn out of ambition?

We, all of us, were elephants trudging on anthills, oblivious to the destruction underfoot.

Tunji Malu was a fiend, a West African vampire who took glee in cruelty. I'd seen no heart locket on him. Never recovered one from his body. I barely remembered the obeah man's death so I couldn't speak for him. But the paper mage was dead. Was that justice? Sure, I couldn't claim she was a good person. She never showed remorse or hesitation like Emily. But did she deserve to die?

I, Cisco Suarez, could easily have been killed during my zombie service. One of my many marks might've gotten the jump on me, or Laurent Baptiste could've succeeded in his ambush. Then I would have fallen, just as Kita had, while under the will of another.

I won't lie. It fucked me up to think that I killed people who could've been me. I knew now there was no right or wrong about it. Just happenstance. But I would never forgive myself.

What did I tell you about heartstrings?

An SUV pulled to the curb and Evan Cross exited the driver's seat. I stood up from the merry-go-round, but the passenger door didn't open. I could see them inside, though.

Shadows.

Evan walked through the gate of the neighborhood park and met me in the playground. It was a weekday, lunchtime, so we had the place to ourselves.

"Did you hear?" he asked, slapping me on the shoulder.

I pulled my eyes away from the figure behind the closed passenger window. "Hear what?"

"The promotion. It's the same position, really, but the DROP team's being overseen by the mayor's office now."

"I saw you on TV."

He nodded. "I'm a fighter of corruption now. The misconduct was so isolated, it doesn't even make the police look bad. Sergeant Garcia was the only cop arrested. That bastard was basically a fixer for the commissioner. The fallout is hitting the business and political worlds harder. Rudi resigned and will be facing charges. Other businesses are under the microscope." The lieutenant puffed his chest out and managed a rare smile. For the first time he wasn't wearing his guns. The sunglasses had stayed, of course.

It was good to see my friend on the right side of things. He'd been under fire—vampire coercion, political plays, investment fraud—but Evan had dodged every bullet. I believed it was because he was a man of principle. Sure, political realities often compromised those principles, but in the end he did what was right. I was proud of him.

A sneaky little thought whispered that Evan had only used the evidence to curry favor for himself, but I shut that cynical poison down hard. I now admitted that I had to trust *some* people in this world. The least I could do was give them the benefit of the doubt until they proved otherwise.

We traded small talk for a while, but it was obvious my friend was just stalling.

"So," I started, glancing at the SUV again. "I know I'm not really free and clear of the law, but with Rudi out of the way, I'm no longer Public Enemy Number One."

Evan grinned. "No one's searching for you, Cisco. The fiascos at City Hall and the commissioner's house are being chalked up to drug disputes within Rudi's circle. He might try for a deal, but he doesn't have anyone to give up, much less you. I think you're safe walking the streets of Miami again."

I nodded away the details. "That's what I'm getting at. We had a deal: Put this manhunt behind us, and I get to meet Fran. That's why you're here now. That's why we're meeting in a playground. Except Emily and Fran haven't gotten out of the car."

His face lost all joviality. "Fran's not in the car, Cisco."

"What?"

"She's in school."

"I thought we agreed this was important enough—"

"Emily is livid with you," he blurted out, kicking at a divot in the grass. He put his hands on his hips and looked into the distance with a sigh. "She can't forgive you for killing Kita."

I'd been through it before with them. They knew about the pull of spellcraft. The heartstone. They knew how and why things went down. Instead of entering the same fray, I let the steam escape my lips and said, "That's still my daughter living in your house."

Evan bit down and removed his sunglasses. "Time, then. Give her more time. That's all I ask."

I watched the grass blow in the distance. "Haven't I given enough of that?"

After a few moments of silence, Evan set his jaw. "Time, then." He nodded lightly to reassure himself, flicked his sunglasses on, and hurried to the car.

I know I have a habit of making things worse, but I followed.

Emily saw me at the sidewalk and turned her head away. I banged on the glass just as Evan closed his door. He looked up and shook his head in disappointment.

I banged again. Emily didn't move but my friend lowered the passenger window halfway.

Emily had been crying. Again. I was a reminder of everything messed up in her life, even what wasn't my fault. But I was also a reminder of the good. What was Fran if not that?

"I want you to know the Covey's done," I told her. Even though she didn't look, she was listening to me. "Disbanded for good. You're one of the lucky ones with a second chance. As long as we're alive, we all have another chance."

She wiped her eyes but didn't respond. I couldn't see into her heart, but I knew she wasn't mine anymore. This was about something more. Evan fought off a bitter frown and started the car.

"Also," I said, giving them pause. "I want you to know, Emily, that I forgive you for everything that happened, just as I hope you can forgive me one day. Everything you took part in—the lies, the plots, the killing—none of it was you."

She sniffled and studied her hands. "You don't know who I am," she said softly. Emily nodded to her husband and they drove away.

I frowned. Emily was wrong. Our life together may have been a lie, but I knew exactly who she was.

She was an animist. A weapon of light, designed against me, aimed specifically at my weakness. But she was more than that too. Stronger. At some point she had fought back. Resisted. Relegated herself to a passive role in the Covey. That proved there was good inside her. She would see that too, one day. As Evan said, it was only a matter of time.

Time.

The playground was empty, as it had been before they met me. It seemed peaceful then. Now when I looked around, I was unsettled. This life—this *dream*—it was so far away. Unattainable.

I scuffed my alligator boot on the sidewalk, settled my heart, and jumped in my truck.

The Everglades was peaceful today. I wasn't bothered by the bumps in the path or the mosquitoes nipping at me. My animal spies reported no strange activity. My arm was healing up nicely except for marked stiffness and what was sure to be a scar cutting through the Nordic tattoo. As I returned to my dank hideaway in the middle of the day, I wanted nothing more than to curl up on my bedroll and sleep for a week.

A skeletal apparition in Spanish armor coalesced. His

burning red eyes glowed with hunger.

"What news?" he asked.

"The commissioner's screwed. The police arrested the sergeant. I'll let the detectives clean up whatever dots they connect."

The skull nodded. "And the elemental?"

"I don't care about him. Connor's the only one I want."

An impatient hiss escaped the spirit's being. His eyes flared. "Our *bargain* covers full justice for your family. The vampire is dead. The Covey is broken. Every strike of your sword adds to the list of enemies. This is a deeper web than we agreed upon, brujo. It is too complicated for my tastes."

I met his gaze. "On the contrary, everything is much simpler now. The gangbangers and businessmen, the police and the Covey and the ghosts, they were all cogs in the greater machine. Henchmen. All of that was noise. Now I have a laser focus on the jinn. Help me take him down, and you're free."

The wraith drew his head up, considered the terms, then vanished.

-Finn

If you're reading this, it means you demand more from your urban fantasy. Bullets and fireballs are a riot, but they're nothing without a layered cast of characters and realistic plot drivers. *Black Magic Outlaw* is my stab at a cut above the rest: non-stop action, true friends banding against impossible odds, and themes that hopefully make you put the book down and ponder, if even for only a minute.

My writing process demands quality control at every step of development. I hope you agree *Black Magic Outlaw* is the premium product I strive to make it. Unfortunately, doubling down on originality and quality in an on-demand world has drawbacks. It's simply impossible for me to get you a brand-new novel every month or two. The process takes time.

That's where you come in. If you want to be a part of building a better book, consider one or all of the following shows of support. The best part? These displays of true fandom don't cost you a penny.

- Join the Outlaw Underground, our private Facebook group. (www.facebook.com/groups/dominofinnfans/)

- Leave an all-too-important review where you bought the book. Each one helps more than you know.

- Recommend this book to your friends. Link it on social media.

- Join my reader group newsletter, get a free Black Magic Outlaw story, and hear from me only when I have new releases or important news. You'll never miss another launch sale again. (dominofinn.com/newsletter/)

Simple, right? Five minutes of your time makes a world of difference to me and Cisco. Thank you for your heartfelt support. I'll keep writing as long as you keep reading.

- Domino Finn

Also by Domino Finn

<u>AFTERLIFE ONLINE</u>
Reboot
Black Hat
Trojan
Deadline

<u>Shade City</u>

<u>SYCAMORE MOON</u>
The Seventh Sons
The Blood of Brothers
The Green Children

About the Author

Domino Finn is a hardened urban fantasy author, media rebel, and Doctor of Wikipedia Studies. (Pro Tip: Lab coats make you look official.)

His stories are equal parts spit, beer, and blood, and are notable for treating weighty issues with a supernatural veneer. If Domino has one rallying cry for the world, it's that fantasy is serious business.

Take a stand at DominoFinn.com